Nowhere to Turn

NOWHERE TO TURN

A ROBYN HUNTER MYSTERY

NORAH McCLINTOCK

MINNEAPOLIS

First U.S. edition published in 2012 by Lerner Publishing Group, Inc.

Darby Creek
A division of Lerner Publishing Group, Inc.
241 First Avenue North
Minneapolis, MN 55401 U.S.A.

Website address: www.lernerbooks.com

The image in this book is used with the permission of: Front
cover: © MILpictures by Tom Weber/Digital Vision/Getty
Images.

Main body text set in Janson Text Lt Std 11.5/15.
Typeface provided by Linotype AG.

Library of Congress Cataloging-in-Publication Data

McClintock, Norah.
    Nowhere to turn / by Norah McClintock.
        p.   cm. — (Robyn Hunter mysteries ; #6)
    ISBN: 978-0-7613-8316-1 (lib. bdg. : alk. paper)
    [1. Mystery and detective stories. 2. Stealing—Fiction.
    3. Dating (Social customs)—Fiction.] I. Title.
    PZ7.M478414184Np 2012
    [Fic]—dc23   2011034341

Manufactured in the United States of America
1 – BP – 7/15/12

To my family

CHAPTER **ONE**

M y father gave me an odd look as he dropped the receiver of the kitchen phone into its cradle. "Aren't you going to be late?" he said, reaching for the coffeepot to refill his mug.

"I've got plenty of time," I said. "I'm meeting Morgan—"

"—downstairs at La Folie. I know." La Folie is the gourmet restaurant that occupies the ground floor of the building my dad owns. He lives on the third floor and rents out apartments on the second floor. "Why doesn't she just come up here? Is it something I said?"

"No, it's something Fred said." Fred Smith is the owner of La Folie. "He promised her a double latte on the house anytime." There's nothing Morgan loves more than double lattes. Except boys—oh yes, and shopping.

"Ah," my father said. He gave me an odd look as he sipped his coffee.

"Something wrong, Dad?"

"No. Why?"

"You're looking at me funny."

"Am I?"

"If it's about Mom—"

I am strictly forbidden from discussing my mother's personal life with my father. My parents had been separated for three years, divorced for one, and my mom had just agreed to marry financial analyst and all-round nice guy Ted Gold. In fact, she and Ted had just left on a two-week vacation to celebrate their engagement. I was staying with my dad while she was gone.

"It isn't about your mother. I was just thinking how quickly you've grown up, Robbie."

He sounded convincingly wistful. I should have known better.

. . .

Morgan Turner, one of my two best friends in the whole world, was sitting serenely at a booth near the window while La Folie's waitstaff swirled around her. The restaurant was doing a brisk Saturday morning brunch business.

"What can I get you, Robyn?" asked Carmine, one of the servers, as I slid in opposite Morgan.

"Nothing, thanks. We're not staying."

"Yes, we are," Morgan said. "At least until I finish this." She raised the giant latte in front of her, took a tiny sip, and settled back against the leather booth. "You know what I wish? I wish I didn't have to spend one more minute in some musty old library poring over stupid books I'm not even interested in, just to fulfill the requirements of some curriculum writer who probably hasn't seen the inside of a high school since before we were born."

Morgan and I had been paired up for a school project. I could see I was in for a barrel of fun.

She took another sip. "You know what else I wish?"

"No." And I wasn't sure I wanted to.

"I wish someone would shoo that girl away. She looks like a junior bag lady. I think her nose is making a grease mark on the glass."

I turned to look and was startled by the face pressed against La Folie's front window.

"Beej," I muttered. Short for B.J. I had no idea what B.J. was short for. Beej was a street kid I had met the previous autumn. When she spotted me, she smiled and waved—which made me instantly suspicious.

"You *know* her?" Morgan said. Her eyes widened in horror. "Oh God. She's coming in. Who is she, Robyn? Please tell me she isn't one of those people from the homeless shelter." She meant the shelter where I volunteered with my boyfriend, Ben.

"She's a friend of Nick's," I said.

Nick was my ex-boyfriend—that is, assuming he'd ever been my boyfriend in the first place. I wasn't sure about that anymore. He had disappeared a few weeks before Christmas but had recently reappeared. Or so I'd heard.

"Nick?" Morgan said, suddenly interested. "Has he called you? Have you seen him?"

"No," I said. "I haven't talked to him. I don't know where he's staying, and he sure hasn't bothered to contact me."

I told myself that I didn't care, but it was a lie. I was furious with him for walking out without a word of explanation. I had promised myself that if I ever saw him again, I'd let him know exactly what I thought.

"Sorry I asked," Morgan said. Her eyes skipped to the door. "Uh-oh. She's headed this way."

Beej definitely did not fit the profile of a typical La Folie customer. She was wearing faded jeans, a beat-up army jacket, and a wool hat with earflaps. A bulging backpack was slung over one shoulder. She loped toward us, oblivious to the looks of La Folie's clientele, and dropped down into the booth beside Morgan. Morgan wrinkled her nose and shifted over.

"Hey, Robyn, long time no see," Beej said, as if she'd actually missed me. That made me even more suspicious. Beej had always given me the impression that she regarded me as a prissy, spoiled, rich (by her standards) kid. She wriggled free of her backpack, unzipped one of the pockets, and pulled out a CD jewel case, which she shoved across the table to me.

"What's that?" I said.

She gave me a look, as if she was trying to assess exactly how stupid I was. "What does it look like?" she said.

"You burned some music for me?"

"*Right*," she said.

"Photos? One of your film projects?"

I hated to admit it, because I wasn't any fonder of Beej than she was of me, but she was actually a really good photographer. She spent every penny she could earn or scrounge on her cameras. She had even won a couple of awards at a downtown youth center for her work. She also made short films. She'd done one on street kids that had aired on a local TV station. "It's a DVD," she said.

"About what?"

"Nick."

I shoved it back across the table.

"Ancient history," I said.

"More like breaking news," Beej said. "I just made it."

Morgan examined the DVD with interest. "You made a movie about Nick?"

Beej glared at her—she and Morgan had never had the pleasure of meeting—snatched the DVD, and slapped it on the table in front of me.

"You have to watch it," she said.

Uh-huh. I hadn't seen Nick in months, and all of a sudden he was sending Beej to find me and give me a DVD that I had to watch? What was on it—an apology? Well, if he wanted to say he was sorry, he was going to have to do it in person. I didn't touch the DVD. I didn't even glance at it. Instead, I reached for my coat. Beej shook her head in disgust.

"You haven't changed a bit," she said.

I pulled the coat on and stood up.

"We have to get to the library," I said to Morgan.

Morgan sighed and, for once, didn't argue. She waved Carmine over and asked for a to-go cup.

"Believe me," Beej said. "I wouldn't be here if it wasn't important. Nick's in trouble."

It kept getting better.

"What kind of trouble?" Morgan said.

"Whatever it is, it's not my problem," I said. "Come on, Morgan."

"Do me a favor," Beej said, standing up. "Watch the DVD. There's a phone number inside the case where you can leave me a message." She shouldered her backpack.

I waited until she was gone before I turned to Morgan.

"Can we go now?" I said.

"I'll be just a sec." Carmine was coming toward the table with a to-go cup, but I couldn't wait any longer. I didn't want to be anywhere near that DVD. I headed for the door. "Wait," Morgan called.

But by then, I was stepping out onto the street. Who did Nick think he was? He'd told me he loved me, and then he'd just vanished. Two months later, I'd heard he was back in town, but he hadn't even called. And now he needed my help?

Right.

.   .   .

"I guess you don't want to talk about it," Morgan said a little later at the library.

"You guess right," I said. I looked at the computer screen and jotted down the call number of a book for our project.

"I wonder what kind of trouble Nick is in," Morgan said. She was sitting at the workstation next to mine and was supposed to be doing the same thing I was doing. But as far as I could tell, she hadn't even started searching the library catalog. "Do you think it's serious?"

I'd been wondering about that, too, ever since we'd left the restaurant. Beej's news had thrown me. Nick, in trouble—again—after all the progress he'd made? He had served time in both closed custody (where they lock the doors and don't let you out, just like prison) and open custody (where they let you out for specific purposes, such as going to school). But he had been getting his life back together. Before he vanished, he'd started going to school again and had been washing dishes part-time at La Folie. My dad had let him have an apartment on the second floor of his building. And I'd been crazy about him . . .

But that was then. I told myself over and over that he wasn't my problem anymore.

"The AV department is on the fifth floor," Morgan said. "We could take a break and watch that DVD."

"First of all," I said, "how can we take a break when we haven't done any work yet? Second, we don't have the DVD. I left it at the restaurant."

Morgan dipped into her backpack. "Ta-da!" she said, waving the DVD case. "Come on. Want to take a look?"

"What I want, Morgan, is to get this assignment done. It counts for 20 percent of our final grade, and I don't particularly want to have to work on it over March break."

"But Nick—"

"Why are you so interested in Nick all of a sudden?" I spoke louder than I had intended, and the librarian at the information desk gave me a sharp look.

"You don't even like him," I whispered. "You're the one who kept telling me to forget about him."

"I just thought—"

I snatched the DVD out of her hand and tossed it into the trash. It landed with a satisfying thud.

"There," I said. "Now can we get to work?"

We spent the next several hours gathering information for our project.

"If we get together again tomorrow and really focus, we can probably finish an outline," I said.

Morgan quietly agreed. She was being uncharacteristically subdued.

"Okay, I'm sorry I snapped at you,' I said.

"It's not your fault. You have unresolved issues with Nick."

"Trust me. They're resolved."

Morgan gave me a look that told me she didn't believe that for a second.

"Ben and Billy will be here soon," she said. "I'm going to freshen up. Coming?"

I shook my head. "I'll wait for you here."

While Morgan was gone, I couldn't help but think about Nick. If he had sent Beej to find me, then whatever mess he had landed himself in had to be big. But how was that my problem? Nick wasn't part of my life. He wasn't my boyfriend anymore. Ben was. Nick was nothing.

The elevator doors opened at the far end of the cavernous main floor of the library. A janitor trundled out his cleaning cart, beginning a circuit of the area, ducking down to scoop up trash and recycling bins and dump their contents into his cart. In a couple of minutes Nick's DVD would be history. I wouldn't have to think about it ever again.

I placed all the books Morgan and I had used in the middle of the table so that they could be reshelved. Then I heard the click of wheels. Behind me, the janitor bent down and picked up the trash bin closest to the computers where Morgan and I had been working earlier.

"Wait!" I cried.

The janitor turned to look at me. So did almost everyone else in the vicinity. I ran over to the cleaning cart.

"I threw something away by accident," I said and thrust my hand into the basket, which fortunately, contained nothing gross. The janitor didn't say a word. He tipped the rest of the contents into a container on his cart, replaced the liner, and moved on. When I turned to retrieve my backpack, Morgan was grinning at me through a fresh application of lipstick. To her credit, she said nothing.

. . .

We ended up going to Ben's house, where Billy and Morgan got to see Ben's brand-new baby half sister for the first time. Billy was mesmerized. He was also in awe of the ease with which Ben lifted her from her basket and held her in the crook of his arm. Billy's sister was expecting her first baby. Maybe Billy was trying to imagine himself in the role of doting uncle.

We ordered pizza (vegan, otherwise Billy wouldn't touch it) and watched a movie before Ben drove us all home. He dropped Billy off first, then Morgan, and finally pulled up in front of my father's building.

"You were pretty quiet tonight," he said. "Is everything okay?"

"Everything's fine," I said. But the truth was that I couldn't have told him a thing about the movie we'd spent two hours watching. "Morgan and I were assigned a big project that we want to finish before March break, which means we're going to have to work on it all day tomorrow."

"I know that feeling," Ben said sympathetically. He leaned over and kissed me on the cheek. "I'll call you tomorrow and see how you're doing," he said, and kissed me again.

It was silent in my dad's loft when I got upstairs. His keys were on the counter in the kitchen and his coat was on a hanger. He must have made an early night of it.

I dug the DVD out of my backpack; popped it into our DVD player, taking care to keep the volume low; and pulled a chair up close.

I had thought I was prepared for what I was about to see, but when Nick's face appeared on the screen, I knew I was wrong.

CHAPTER **TWO**

Nick's thick black hair was longer than it had been the last time I'd seen him. He looked thinner too and tired, as if he hadn't slept in days. The hairline scar that ran from the bridge of his nose to the bottom of his right ear stood out against his pale skin. He was sitting in an armchair in a brightly lit room. His first words were "What's the point? They caught me with some of the stuff on me. They have the crowbar. I'm screwed.

"They say they'll make a deal with me if I tell them what I did with the rest of it. But they're going to lock me up, Beej. With all the trouble I've been in, they're going to lock me up for sure."

"That's why you should make a record of what happened," Beej said.

"What's the point?" Nick said again. I moved a hand toward the screen to touch his face, then pulled it back when I realized what I was doing.

"The cops make a record of everything," Beej said. "You should make a record too while everything's fresh in your mind. It always helps to talk things out."

Nick shook his head.

"Okay," Beej said. "So maybe I'll get into Sundance with my documentary about Nick D'Angelo and his many brushes with the law."

If she was trying to lighten his mood, it didn't work. Nick sank back in his chair and stared close-mouthed into the camera. He hadn't sent Beej to deliver the DVD to me. He hadn't even wanted her to make it.

"Did you do it?" Beej said.

Nick stared sullenly at the camera and didn't answer.

"Why don't you start by telling what happened to Mr. Schuster?" Beej said.

Nick and I had met Mort Schuster last summer. I had been volunteering at an animal shelter, and Nick was in a special anger management program there. The program was supposed to teach him and some other kids patience and self-control by training them to work with dogs that had behavior problems of their own. The human participants learned how to control their frustration by helping the canine participants overcome their problems so that they could be adopted rather than put down. Nick had trained a big black beast named Orion. When the program ended, Schuster, a volunteer at the shelter, adopted Orion. Then, because Mr. Schuster wasn't able to walk long distances and because he had grown fond of Nick, he hired Nick as a dog walker.

"You already know what happened," Nick said.

"Humor me," Beej said, her patience wearing thin.

Nick stared at the camera again. "I got back to the house after walking Orion and found Mr. Schuster lying on the floor. He couldn't move. I called 9-1-1. They took him to the hospital."

"Did Mr. Schuster say anything to you before they took him away?"

"Dog," Nick said. "He said, 'Dog.' It was the only word he said."

"He wanted you to look after Orion for him, right?" Beej said.

Nick shrugged. "I guess."

"Then what happened?"

"This is a waste of time."

"Do you have any better ideas?"

Nick scowled at the camera. Beej held it steady on him until he spoke again.

"Mr. Schuster's family showed up at the house the next night—his son and daughter-in-law and their kids." He shook his head. "I wasn't expecting that. Orion was sleeping in his room. I was on the couch."

"You were staying at Mr. Schuster's?" Beej said.

"While he was in the hospital, yeah," Nick said. "I figured he'd appreciate it if I looked after Orion. But his family acted like I was there to rob the place. The son, Elliot, started yelling at me. He wanted to know who I was and what I was doing in his dad's house. I was pretty sure he was going to call the cops. I thought his wife would say something, but she didn't. She just stood there and let Elliot give me the third degree."

"What did you tell him?"

Nick didn't answer.

Beej sighed. "Okay. And then what happened?"

"It was crazy. Elliot was quizzing me, Orion was barking up in his room, and then Claudia—that's the wife—decided to go upstairs. If I'd known what she was going to do, I would have stopped her. She heard Orion barking. She must have been able to tell which room he was in. She should have known better, but she barged into his room. Then we heard her scream, and Elliot charged up the stairs. I'm not sure what happened, except that Orion bit her. At least, that's what she said.

"It wasn't serious. There was no blood or anything. Knowing Orion, it was more like a nip. He probably thought she was an intruder. He only ever met her that one time. And it didn't help that she got so worked up." He shook his head again. "I tried to get everyone to calm down, but every time Orion moved, Claudia freaked out, and that got Orion going all over again. Every time I gave the command and got him to be quiet, she'd start in, screaming at me to keep the dog away from her. And then he'd start barking again. It was a vicious circle."

He sounded exasperated. "They're terrified of him. Finally, Claudia started screaming at Elliot to call Animal Control. She said she didn't care what Mr. Schuster said about Orion—"

"What did Mr. Schuster say?" Beej said.

"That he's a good dog. That there was no reason to be afraid of him. He said that all the time, you know, because he's so big and has such a deep bark. Claudia said it was obvious he was a vicious dog. She said he should be put down."

Anger flashed in his eyes, and that scared me. Nick did stupid things when he got angry.

"Then what?" Beej prompted.

"Mr. Schuster's granddaughter said that it would be wrong to do anything to Orion without telling him. In the end, Elliot told me to put Orion in the basement." He looked disgusted. "Anyway, they must have talked to Mr. Schuster at the hospital the next day, because when I went to the house to check on Orion, Elliot hired me to look after him, walk him every day. But they insisted on keeping him in the basement."

"Then?"

"Then nothing."

"C'mon, Nick." Beej was working hard to get the story out of him, but he wasn't making it easy. "Something happened . . ."

"Yeah," Nick said. "Three days later, Elliot fired me."

"Why?"

"You know why."

Beej sighed again. "Okay, then what *happened*?"

Nick stared at the lens.

"What do you think?" he said.

"You got mad, right? Nick?"

His eyes shifted to the floor. "Maybe I did a few things I shouldn't have."

"And then?"

"A few days later, the cops busted me for breaking and entering and theft. Okay? Satisfied?" His temper flared again, and he stalked out of the frame. Beej switched her camera off. The end.

I stared at the blank screen. Breaking and entering? Theft?

I popped the DVD out of the player—and almost dropped it when I turned and saw my father standing behind me in pajama bottoms and a T-shirt, his hair mussed from sleeping. I wasn't sure how much of Beej's film he had seen, but I was sure he'd seen at least some of it. He didn't look terribly surprised.

I thought about Beej peering through the window of La Folie . . . as if she'd had a pretty good idea she'd find me there.

I thought about my dad in the kitchen earlier that morning, hanging up the phone and giving me that peculiar look.

"She called here, didn't she?" I said.

He didn't ask who I meant.

"What did she say, Dad?"

"She wanted to know where she could find you."

"Why didn't she just ask for me?"

"She said she wanted to give you something, but she was afraid you'd hang up on her."

"So you told her I was going to be at La Folie?"

He nodded. I glanced at the TV.

"Did you see the whole thing while you were standing there?" I said.

"I caught the end of it."

"What should I do?"

"Is there anything you *can* do?" my dad asked. "If you want, I could ask around, see how serious it is."

I set the DVD on top of the player and headed for my room—well, the room that my dad calls mine when he's not calling it the guest room. As I opened the door, I heard Nick's voice again in the living room: "What's the point?"

. . .

"Do you think we could go inside before I freeze my butt off?" Morgan said. She stamped her feet and hugged herself with mittened hands.

"You go ahead," I said. "I'll be up in a while."

Morgan eyed me suspiciously. She had surprised me by showing up at the library ten minutes early instead of her usual ten minutes late. Beej, on the other hand, was nearly half an hour late, which left me unsympathetic to Morgan's complaints. I had been freezing my butt off for at least three times longer than she had.

"What's going on?" she said. "Who are you waiting for?"

"Who says I'm waiting for anyone?" I said. The DVD case Beej had given me had her number inside.

I had called the number and left a message telling her where and when to meet me. So far, she was a no-show.

"You're meeting that girl, aren't you?" Morgan said.

"What girl?"

"*That* girl," she said, pointing. Beej was swinging down the street toward us, wearing the same clothes she'd had on the day before. "You watched it, didn't you?" Morgan said.

I nodded as Beej came to a stop in front of me.

"So?" Beej said. She didn't apologize for being late.

I glanced at Morgan. "Why don't you go inside and get warm?" I said. "I'll catch up with you soon."

She crossed her arms over her chest and stayed where she was. Well, she was my best friend. I turned to Beej.

"He has a lawyer, right?"

"Nick needs a lawyer?" Morgan said.

"He's got some public defender," Beej said. "But you know what they're like—overworked, underpaid, and not very good. Otherwise, they'd be making the big bucks."

She obviously didn't know what she was talking about. My mother had represented Nick in the past, and she was a very good lawyer. But I let it slide.

Beej continued. "And since the cops found him with stolen property and the crowbar used to pry open the side door, I bet the lawyer's going to push him to plead guilty."

"Nick stole something?" Morgan asked.

"He didn't do it," Beej said.

"Did he tell you that?" I asked.

Beej looked angrily at me.

"In the DVD you gave me, you asked him, but he didn't answer," I said. "Did he come out and tell you he didn't do it?"

"Not exactly," she admitted. "But I only talked to him that one time. Besides, I know Nick. He's not a thief."

"If he didn't do it," Morgan said, "why'd he have stolen property on him?"

Beej ignored her. "Do you really think Nick would steal from Mr. Schuster?" she asked me. "When he was in the *hospital*?"

"They arrested Nick for stealing from Mr. Schuster?" I said. As far as I knew, the only thing Nick had ever stolen was some money. That had happened a long time ago, back in middle school, and his stepbrother Joey had been the one behind it. But that didn't mean that if I tried, I couldn't imagine him stealing to get even for something— like, say, for being fired. But stealing from Mr. Schuster?

"You don't believe me, do you?" Beej said.

"Even if I did believe you, what difference would it make? I wasn't there. There's nothing I can do."

"You could go and see Nick. You could talk to him."

"What good would that do?"

"I'm worried about him," Beej said. "He's been different ever since he got back to town. Quieter than usual. You saw the DVD. You saw what he's like. Getting him to say anything is like pulling teeth. I'm afraid of what he might do."

"If he wants my help, he can ask me himself."

"He acts like he doesn't want anyone's help," Beej said. "He'll kill me when he finds out I told you."

"In other words," I said sourly, "not only does he *not* want my help, but he doesn't even want to see me."

Beej shook her head. "You don't get it," she said. "You know Nick's record. The cops'll lock him up for sure. Someone has to do something."

"He doesn't hide his problems from you," I said. "He obviously considers you his friend. Why don't you do something?"

"I *am* his friend," Beej said. "But I can't get near him."

"Why not?"

"Because we were together when he was arrested."

"What do you mean, together?"

"The day before he was arrested, I found out he was sleeping in a warehouse by the docks. I'd assumed he was staying with his aunt, but he wasn't. He was sleeping rough. So I told him he could stay at my place."

"You mean at the squat?" When I'd met Beej last year, she'd been living in an abandoned building. It couldn't have been any warmer than Nick's warehouse.

She shook her head. "I share a house with a bunch of people now. Nick was gonna stay there until he could figure out what to do. But the cops showed up and arrested him. He only got released because his aunt agreed to make sure he showed up at court and stuff.

"When his aunt caught me at her place making that DVD, she threw me out," Beej continued. "She won't even let me talk to him. How am I supposed to help him?"

"What was stolen?" I said.

"Mr. Schuster's coin collection. It was worth a lot of money."

"Define 'a lot.'"

When she told us, Morgan whistled softly.

"And they found the collection on Nick?" I said.

"They found a few coins in his backpack," Beej said. "And they found the crowbar at the place where he'd been sleeping. They say it's the one used to pry open Mr. Schuster's side door. I know it sounds bad . . ."

"What about Mr. Schuster?" I said. "What happened to him?"

"Nick says he had a stroke. It's too bad. He's a really nice guy."

"You know Mr. Schuster?"

"Sure," Beej said. "Mr. Schuster hired me to walk Orion while Nick was gone."

Nick had disappeared while I was out of town on a school trip. I'd been worried sick. I'd asked everyone I could think of if they'd seen him. I'd even called Mr. Schuster, who'd told me that he didn't know where Nick had gone. I'd tried to track Beej down so I could ask her too, but the couple of times I'd ventured into the dilapidated building she used to call home, there had been no sign of her. But apparently she'd known all along that Nick was leaving. He'd even made arrangements for her to look after Orion, but he hadn't bothered to let me know where he was going or why. A dog was more important to him than I was.

"How is Mr. Schuster?" I said, determined not to let Beej see how hurt I was. "Is he going to be all right?"

"His family won't tell me anything," she said. "I went over there with Nick a couple of times before Elliot fired him. I was nice to them too. I even took some pictures of them for Mr. Schuster, you know, while he was in the hospital. But they know I'm a friend of Nick's so now they treat me like poison. I know he's back at home—that has to be a good sign, right?"

"Maybe. What makes you think *I* can do anything?"

"His aunt and that . . . guy she lives with think Nick messed up again. The cops are positive they've got the right guy. I've done everything I can. You're the only person I could think of that his aunt might let see him. You also know Mr. Schuster. I thought maybe you could find some way to help Nick. I don't know what happened between you two—that's one more thing he won't talk about. But it's obvious you still care about him."

I stared at her. "What makes you say that?"

She shook her head.

"If you didn't care, you wouldn't have watched the DVD," she said. "You wouldn't have called me."

CHAPTER **THREE**

"**Y**ou're going to do it, aren't you?" Morgan said after Beej had left. "You're going to see Nick."

"*We're* going to go and see Nick," I said. "This is your fault. I left that DVD in the restaurant. You had to pick it up and bring it to the library."

"And *you're* the one who fished it out of the garbage. Come on, Robyn. You know you wanted to watch it."

"And you know you want to come with me to see Nick." I didn't know how I would feel once I was face-to-face with Nick again. "I don't think I can do it alone, Morgan."

According to Beej, the judge had placed three conditions on Nick's release. He had to stay at his aunt's house until his court date, he wasn't allowed any contact with Beej, and he wasn't allowed to go near Mr. Schuster or his family. Nick's aunt had made it clear that if Nick violated any of the conditions, she'd call the police. Nick would be held in custody until his trial. I wondered if she would let me see him. If she did, would Nick even talk to me?

Nick's aunt wasn't home. Her live-in boyfriend, Glen, answered the door. Glen was a cop. He didn't like Nick. The feeling was mutual.

"Is Nick here?" I said.

Glen eyed me critically. Like a lot of cops, he knew my father. "Your dad's a smart guy," he said. "Your mom must be pretty smart too. She's a lawyer, right?"

I nodded.

"So how can a girl with such smart parents be dumb enough to waste time on a loser like Nick? They're going to put him away this time. They got him on breaking and entering, theft, assault . . ."

"Assault?" Becj hadn't mentioned that.

"First, he steals from a sick old man," Glen said. "Then, once he's been released, he forces his way back into the old man's house. When the daughter-in-law tries to stop him, Nick assaults her." He shook his head. "He's breaking his aunt's heart. He never learned how to control himself. I keep telling her, I've seen dozens of kids like him, and sooner or later, they all self-destruct."

"Can I talk to him?" I said.

Glen studied me for a moment. "What the heck," he said. "If Bev were here, she'd let you. I think she was hoping you could change him." He snorted.

Glen opened the door and let us in. "Five minutes, no more. He's in the basement. We figured if he has to hang around here, he might as well clean up the place, make himself useful. It's through that door."

Morgan and I unbuttoned our coats and headed for the basement.

"What a jerk," Morgan muttered in my ear.

The main part of the basement was an entertainment room with a bar, a sofa, and a big-screen TV. But Nick was in the unfinished area, which contained a washer, a dryer, and a wall of shelves. He was kneeling on the concrete floor, sorting through a box of clothes. I stopped in the doorway between the rec room and where Nick was, unable to make myself go any farther. I gripped the doorframe to steady myself.

When Nick saw me, he sprang to his feet. "What are you doing here?"

Some foolish part of me had been hoping that he would be happy to see me, but he obviously wasn't. He looked taller than I remembered, maybe because he'd lost so much weight since he'd been gone. I remembered what Beej had said. He'd been sleeping rough. He probably hadn't been eating properly either.

My mouth was dry. I felt like I was choking.

"Beej said—" I began.

He shook his head in disgust.

"I knew it was a mistake to talk to her stupid camera," he said.

He looked down at the ring I was wearing. Ben had given it to me. Ever since I'd found out that Nick was back in town, I had been wondering how much he knew.

The look he gave me answered that question. But how did he feel? Peering at him, I couldn't tell. Maybe he'd decided before he left town that he wasn't interested in me anymore. Maybe that was why he had left.

"It sounds like you're in trouble," I said. "Again," I added—because of the cold way he was looking at me, because I was angry with him for abandoning me, because I wanted to hurt him as much as he had hurt me.

"I didn't ask you to come over here," he said. "So why don't you leave?"

I stayed put.

"I mean it, Robyn."

Our eyes locked. I saw nothing but fury in his. He raised a fist and hammered it against the metal shelving. Empty jars rattled. Morgan yelped in surprise.

"Hey!" Glen roared from upstairs. "What's going on down there?"

I looked at Nick. Maybe Glen was right. Maybe he was out of control. Maybe he had lashed out in rage when Elliot fired him. Maybe he was self-destructing.

I drew in a deep breath. Even though I was angry with him, I didn't want anything bad to happen to him.

"It's nothing," I yelled back to Glen. "I just tripped, that's all." I turned back to Nick. "I don't understand what's going on. Things were going so well for you! You had your own place. You had a job. You were in school. What happened?"

He glanced at my ring again. His eyes drilled into me.

"When did you start seeing that guy?" he said.

"What?"

"You heard me. When?"

"You weren't here, Nick. You left, remember?"

"I would have waited for you, Robyn."

"Then why did you—" Morgan began. She stopped when Nick and I both spun around to look at her. "You begged me to come, Robyn," she pointed out. I gave her another look. "Fine," she said. She retreated to the other room, dropped down onto the sofa, and made a big show of zipping her lips.

I turned back to Nick. Just seeing him brought back all the pain I had felt.

"I would never have left you the way you left me," I said. "Not for anything."

He stared angrily at me. Unless one of us calmed down, this was going to end up in a fight.

"We both did what we did," I continued. "I didn't come to talk about the past. I came because Beej said you were in trouble and because we used to be friends."

"Friends?" he said. "Is that what we were?" He shook his head. "I don't need your help."

"Come on, Nick. If you didn't do what they say you did—"

"If?"

"Five minutes are up!" Glen bellowed from upstairs.

I didn't move. "You know what I mean. If there's anything I can do—"

Nick stared at me for what seemed like a full minute. "You want to be a *friend*?" He spat out the word. "You want to do something? Okay. You can tell Mr. Schuster it wasn't me. And you can make sure that Orion is okay." I caught a flicker of anguish in his eyes. "Elliot had the phone in his hand, Robyn. He was going to call Animal Control. He was ready to have Orion taken away. But it wasn't his fault. She should have known better."

I took a step toward him. Suddenly all I wanted was to wrap my arms around him and tell him everything was going to be okay. But he ducked back out of my reach and his face grew hard again.

"You think you can do that for me, friend?" he said.

I heard footsteps on the basement stairs. Morgan touched my arm.

"We should go," she said.

I nodded. Tears stung my eyes, but I fought them back as I turned away from him.

"Hey, Robyn?" Nick said.

I turned back.

"Things would never have worked out with us anyway. You and I live in different worlds. Beej is more my type."

CHAPTER **FOUR**

I couldn't get those words out of my mind: *Beej is more my type*.

"You think he's seeing that Beej person?" Morgan said as we walked to the bus stop. "You think that's why she wants to help him so badly?"

"I don't know."

"Do you think he was seeing her while he was still seeing you? I mean, he told her he was leaving town. And they hooked up when he got back."

"I said I don't know, Morgan!" I snapped.

She was silent for a few moments. Then: "Well, it sounds like Billy was right—Nick saw Ben give you that ring."

I felt Ben's ring burning into my skin as she spoke. On Valentine's Day, Ben had taken me to a nice restaurant, where we'd had a table by the window. While we were sitting there, Ben had presented me with a small box, lifted the ring out, and slipped it onto my finger. Later, I'd found out that Billy had spotted Nick standing across the street from that same restaurant. Billy said he was pretty sure that Nick had been staring at us.

"What are you going to do?" Morgan said.

"About what?"

"About Nick."

"Who says I'm going to do anything?"

She sighed. "You can kid yourself if you want to, Robyn. But you can't kid me. Right this minute you're thinking about what you can do to help him. You're probably even thinking that if you *do* help him, maybe the two of you can get back together."

"Don't be ridiculous," I said. "You heard what he said. I'm not his type. Besides, I'm with Ben now."

"So you're not going to help him? You're not going to do anything?"

"I'm going to be a friend," I said. "I'm going to do what he asked. I'm going to talk to Mr. Schuster."

"Uh-huh. Are you going to tell Ben?"

"There's nothing to tell."

"You want me to go with you?" Morgan said after a few moments of silence.

I shook my head. "I have no idea how sick Mr. Schuster is or whether I'll even be able to see him. I'll meet you back at the library, okay?"

But that wasn't the real reason I wanted to go to Mr. Schuster's house alone. The truth was, I wanted to find out what was going on and—Morgan was right—I wanted to help Nick. I'd made up my mind after watching Beej's DVD. I wanted to help him despite what he thought about me, because it just didn't add up.

Nick had been in trouble before, almost always because he had difficulty controlling his temper. And sure, sometimes when his temper got the better of him, he did incredibly stupid things. But no matter how much I thought about it, there was no way I could believe that he would steal from Mr. Schuster.

But—and this was a big but—the police had caught Nick with part of Mr. Schuster's stolen coin collection. Something was going on, something that threatened to get Nick locked up.

Morgan was right about something else too. I told myself it would never happen. I told myself I didn't even want it to happen—that if Nick didn't want me, then I didn't want him, either. But a part of me—I told myself it was just a tiny, silly part—pictured Nick and me together again.

I made a stop on my way to Mr. Schuster's house. As I climbed the steps to his front porch, I was clutching a small paper bag from Kanine Kookies.

A girl about my age swung open the inner door. She seemed surprised to see me.

"Is Mr. Schuster home?" I said.

She peered out uncertainly.

"My name is Robyn," I said. "I volunteered with Mr. Schuster at the animal shelter last summer."

"Oh," she said. "Grandpa told me about you."

"He did?"

"Before he got sick, he used to e-mail me almost every day. That's how we stay in touch."

From somewhere deep inside the house, I heard the rumbling roowf-roowf of a large dog. The girl looked apprehensively over her shoulder. When she turned back to me, her face was white. She looked as terrified as I must have the first time I laid eyes on Schuster's big black dog.

"Is that Orion?" I said, trying to keep my voice light. I have a long and deep-seated fear of dogs. It shouldn't have applied to Orion—after all, I knew him. But I had been alone with him exactly once, months ago.

The girl nodded. "He bit my mom, so my dad put him in the basement. But I don't think he likes it down there."

The girl shook her head. "Grandpa e-mailed me all about Orion. He told me he was a big dog. But I never realized how big until we got here after Grandpa had his stroke. My mother said his last owner gave him to the shelter because he's vicious."

"He had some behavior problems," I admitted. "But he was in a special program at the shelter, and he graduated with flying colors. If he bit your mother, it was probably because he was scared or startled. But he's friendly once you get to know him."

"You mean, you're not afraid of him?" the girl said.

I took my chance to do at least part of what Nick had asked—to check on Orion.

"No, I'm not," I said. I tried to sound matter-of-fact about it.

The girl looked at me with new interest.

"My name is Isobel," she said. "Could you wait here for a minute?" She left the inside door open and ran up the stairs. She was back a few moments later. "Grandpa really wants to see Orion. Do you think you could bring him upstairs?"

"Sure," I said, as if it would be no problem at all. But my heart pounded in my chest. What if Orion didn't listen to me? What if being locked in the basement all this time had made him forget what Mr. Schuster and Nick had taught him?

Isobel stood back to let me inside. I pulled off my boots as Orion's throaty roowf filled the house.

"He barks a lot," Isobel said. "My dad says it's driving him crazy."

"Does anyone take him out for walks?"

Isobel shook her head. "We're all afraid to go near him." She pointed at the door to the basement. "My dad put a barrier at the bottom of the stairs so that he can take food and water downstairs without Orion charging at him." She looked at me again. "Are you sure you want to go down there?"

I was nowhere close to sure. But I had decided to do what Nick had asked, no matter what he thought of me. And if I got a chance to see Mr. Schuster, too, maybe I could even start to get an idea of exactly what had happened.

I opened the Kanine Kookies bag and pulled out a gourmet dog biscuit. Nick used to buy them for Orion when he could afford to. I looked at the basement door and tried to remember everything Nick had told me about dogs in general and about Orion in particular.

First, he had said, dogs get to know people by their scent. Once dogs get to know someone, they remember that person. So theoretically, Orion should remember me.

Second, Nick had said that Orion was really a big softy. If he didn't sense that you were afraid—fear put him on his guard—and if you talked softly but firmly to him, he would be fine. If you approached him with his favorite treat and let him smell that too, he would be your friend for life.

I wasn't exactly eager to put this to the test. But I trusted Nick about Orion, even if I didn't always trust him about other things.

I reached for the doorknob.

"Wait," Isobel cried from the front hall. "The light switch is just inside the door to the left."

My knees trembled. My heart hammered. But I forced myself to smile—as if that would convince Orion I wasn't afraid—and opened the door. The barking below grew more frantic. From the landing, stairs continued down into the darkness. I switched on the light. That must have surprised Orion because he was quiet for a moment. Then he started barking louder than ever.

"Hey, Orion," I said softly. A large piece of plywood had been positioned across the bottom of the stairs. That may have made Elliot Schuster and his family feel safe, but as I crept down toward the barking, I thought about Orion's point of view. Someone had imprisoned him down there, away from his master, away from his regular life. I sure hoped he wouldn't blame me for keeping him locked up.

Roowf-roowf-roowf . . . *blam!*

What the—? I froze.

Blam!

Orion was hurling himself against the plywood barrier. I caught a glimpse of his wild yellow eyes. My instinct was to run back up the stairs and slam the door behind me. But I stayed where I was. *Think of Orion*, I told myself. *Think how he must feel.*

I drew in a trembling breath and spoke Orion's name again while I continued down the stairs. When I got close to the barrier, I extended a trembling hand so that he could catch my scent. I prayed that he wouldn't try to take a chunk out of me. He kept barking, but he sounded slightly less frenzied.

"Hey, Orion," I repeated—soothingly, I hoped. "Hey, boy." Holding my breath, I did what I had seen Nick do a hundred times before. I let him sniff me. Only after that did I reach over the barrier. My fingers grazed Orion's head and I began to scratch behind his left ear. Nick had said he loved that. He was right. Orion stopped barking.

"Good boy," I cooed. "Look what I have for you." I held out the dog biscuit. Orion looked at me, waiting for the signal that Nick always gave him. I nodded. He grabbed the biscuit out of my hand and crunched it. His tail began to wag. "Good dog," I said, reaching over to scratch behind his ear again. This time he didn't bark. I began to believe that I, the most dog-phobic person I knew, could actually handle this beast.

"Sit," I said, gently but firmly, like I'd heard Nick do dozens of times.

To my surprise, the big dog plopped down onto his rear end.

I glanced around and saw a leash hanging from a hook on the wall. I grabbed it, leaned over the barricade, and attached it to Orion's collar.

"Stay," I said. Orion watched me with eager eyes but remained seated as I slid the heavy plywood barrier aside. "Come," I said. Orion trotted contentedly up the stairs beside me.

Isobel was still in the hall, one hand on the front door handle, planning to bolt from the house at the first sign of danger.

"Do you want to get acquainted?" I said.

She looked warily at Orion. Then she inched toward me.

"Don't be afraid," I said. "After all, he's your grand-father's dog." I took one of her hands and held it close to Orion. He sniffed it. "You can pat him if you want to," I said.

Isobel shook her head and pulled her hand away.

"He'll never get to know you if you don't let him."

She looked terrified. But after a moment, she reached out again and gingerly touched the top of Orion's head. His tail wagged.

"See?" I said. "He's not so scary."

Orion roowfed—the sound was as loud and unexpected as a thunderclap. Isobel jumped back.

"Grandpa is upstairs," she said. "He'll understand what you say, but you might not understand him. His doctor says he's doing really well. But the stroke affected his speech."

I took off my coat and set down my backpack, keeping a firm grip on Orion. Isobel led the way up the stairs to a bright, sunny bedroom at the front of the house. I had expected to find Mr. Schuster in bed, but instead, he was sitting in an armchair near the window. A walker stood on the floor beside the chair. He smiled when he saw me, but there was something odd about his expression. It took me a moment to figure out what: only one side of his mouth had curled up. The other side hadn't moved at all.

"Look who's here to see you, Grandpa," Isobel said.

Orion dragged me across the room. I held tight to his leash, afraid that he would jump up on Mr. Schuster. But the big dog seemed to sense that his master wasn't well. He plunked himself down next to Schuster and dropped his massive head onto the old man's knees. Schuster's left hand trembled when he reached out to pat Orion. The dog's tail thumped on the floor. Mr. Schuster looked at me. Tears welled up in his eyes.

"Troop Fred seal," he said.

At least, that's what it sounded like.

CHAPTER **FIVE**

"He's happy to see Orion," Isobel said. "Aren't you, Grandpa?"

Mr. Schuster nodded.

"Bit," he said. "Bit . . . bat . . ." He looked frustrated. Finally, he raised his hand to his face and touched the side of his nose with one finger. His hand shook as he dragged the finger across his cheek. He looked at me intently the whole time, as if he were trying to tell me something. I was almost positive I knew what he meant, but I wasn't sure if I should admit it in front of Isobel.

Isobel picked up a pad of paper from the bedside table, set it on Mr. Schuster's lap, and pressed a pencil into his hand.

"Can you write it, Grandpa?" she said.

I watched Mr. Schuster make a squiggly upward line. The letters he formed were shaky, but I had no trouble reading what he wrote: *Nick?*

I glanced at Isobel.

"It's okay," she said. "I know you know him."

If that was true and if Nick had done all the things Glen had said he'd done, why had she let me into the house?

"I think he wants to know if you've seen Nick," Isobel said. "Don't you, Grandpa?"

Mr. Schuster nodded.

"Yes," I admitted. I looked into Mr. Schuster's watery eyes. "He asked me to check on Orion. He also wanted me to tell you that he didn't do it."

Schuster formed more letters on his notepad: *Where?*

"*Where* is Nick?" I asked. He nodded. "He's staying at his aunt's house until his court date."

Mr. Schuster sank back in his chair.

"Grandpa's tired," Isobel said. "He had physical therapy this morning and speech therapy this afternoon. We should let him rest."

But when I gathered Orion's leash, Schuster grabbed me by the hand. He struggled hard to form just two words. They came out in a trembling whisper, but this time I had no trouble understanding them. He wanted me to come back.

"I will," I said. "I promise."

I kept a tight grip on Orion's leash as I followed Isobel out into the hall, but he kept pulling away from me. He seemed to want to go to the back of the house.

"Orion used to sleep in the back bedroom," Isobel said. "I guess he misses it. My mom and dad are using that room while we're here."

Orion followed me reluctantly down the stairs but balked at the door to the basement.

"Come on, boy," I said, giving the leash a gentle tug.

He dug his heels in, growling and barking. I don't know what was going through his doggy mind, but it was clear that he wanted to stay where he was. Isobel backed away.

"See?" she said, her voice trembling. "He doesn't like it down there. But my dad says if he's going to stay, he has to stay in the basement."

"Orion, *come*," I said. He refused to move. I turned to Isobel. "There's a bag of dog biscuits in my coat pocket. Can you grab me one?"

She was back in a flash and handed me a biscuit. That got Orion's attention. He leaned toward me, waiting to see if I would give him one. But I didn't. Not yet. I held the biscuit out in front of him and used it to wave him through the basement door and down the stairs. When we reached the bottom, I tossed the biscuit to the farthest end of the concrete floor. Orion looked at me. I nodded curtly. He bounded across the floor. Quickly, I replaced the plywood barrier. Orion didn't seem to notice. I retreated upstairs but left the basement light on for him. Isobel stood waiting in the front hall.

"Is your grandpa going to be okay?" I asked while I pulled on my boots.

"He gets really frustrated when he has trouble talk-ing," Isobel said.

"That happens to a lot of people who have strokes," I said. It had happened to my grandmother.

"I know," Isobel said. "I keep telling him that. We all do. And his doctor says that he's doing great in other ways. Grandpa is really strong. He was able to get out of bed almost right away—with help—and his doctor says that's good. His right side is weak, but his left side is fine. He's already getting around upstairs with a walker. The physical therapist says he'll be ready to tackle the stairs any day now. I know Grandpa can't wait. He hates being cooped up like this. I promised him as soon as the doctor said it was okay, we'd go to the mall and people watch."

"That's great," I said. "He's lucky you're here." I considered my next question carefully as I buttoned my coat. "Isobel, how did you know I know Nick? Did your grandfather tell you that in his e-mails too?"

She shook her head. "He told me about Nick and about you, but he never said anything about the two of you being friends."

Friends.

"But upstairs, you said you knew that I knew him."

"Nick had a picture of you in his backpack. It fell out one day when he was getting ready to take Orion for a walk."

Nick had been carrying a picture of me? Even after he'd seen Ben and me together?

"I asked him if it was a picture of his girlfriend," Isobel said. She blushed. "He's so quiet, you know? I was trying to find out if he was seeing anyone."

I held my breath.

"But he said it was just a picture of someone he knew from the animal shelter. That's how I knew he knew you. Then the next couple of times he came over, another girl came with him. She was kind of dirty-looking, but Nick seemed really friendly with her. Is she his girlfriend?"

"I don't know," I said. Nick hadn't even said I was a friend. I was just "someone he knew."

"I thought he was nice," Isobel said. "And I know Grandpa likes him. He told me he'd hired him as a dog walker. He said Nick was really smart."

"Is that all he said?"

"What do you mean?"

"Did he tell you anything about Nick's past?"

"You mean that he'd been in trouble before?" She shook her head. "My dad was really mad when he found out that Grandpa let Nick into the house even though he knew that he had a record."

Isobel walked me to the door.

"You told Grandpa that Nick said he didn't take those coins," she said. "Do you believe that?"

"I know he isn't a thief," I said.

"But the police said—"

"I know it looks bad, Isobel. But I also know Nick. He likes your grandfather. He respects him. I can't believe that he would steal from him."

Isobel looked doubtful.

"What does your grandfather think?" I asked.

"I know he's upset that his coins are missing. They were important to him. He's been a collector forever. At first my dad didn't want to tell him about the theft—Grandpa was in the hospital when it happened. But he needed Grandpa to sign some papers for the insurance, so he had to. I was there when he did. I saw the look on his face. He was so sad when my dad told him what the police had said." She looked at me. "My dad says Nick had probably been waiting for the opportunity to steal from Grandpa."

I could see how someone might think that—someone who didn't know Nick, like Isobel's father, or someone who had a low opinion of him, like Glen. But that didn't make them right. I pulled on my mittens and reached for the doorknob. I had delivered Nick's message. I had checked on Orion. But I hadn't learned any more than Beej's DVD had already told me. I turned back to Isobel. There was one more thing I needed to know—for me this time, not for Nick.

"I heard that Nick got into some kind of argument with your mother. Is that true?"

Isobel nodded.

"Grandpa was really upset about that too," she said. "Nick came over to the house after he got out on bail the first time. Grandpa had just got home from the hospital. My mom was here with him. Nick said he wanted to talk to him, but my mom wouldn't let him in the house. She told him to go away, but he barged into the house anyway. When she tried to stop him, he hit her."

My heart sank. Nick sometimes had trouble controlling his temper, but he'd made a lot of progress with that. I didn't want to believe that he would hit anyone, let alone Mr. Schuster's daughter-in-law. I wished I understood what was going on with him. I wished there was something I could do to make all this trouble go away.

"My mom said he only left when she called 9-1-1," Isobel continued. "The police arrested him again."

I pulled a notebook and pen out of my backpack and scribbled down my cell phone number.

"If you need any help with Orion, call me," I said. "I'd be glad to help."

As I walked to the bus stop, I thought about Nick. Should I try to see him again? Could I bear to after what he had said? What would I do if he came right out and told me that he and Beej had been seeing each other?

Beej.

She was worried about Nick. She was afraid he wasn't going to put up a fight and, much as I hated to agree with her on anything, it looked like she was right: Nick seemed to take it for granted that everyone believed the worst of him. Despite that, Beej was determined to help him. And for that she needed me. She wasn't allowed to see Nick, but I was. She couldn't get near Mr. Schuster's house, but I could. She believed Nick when he said he didn't do it. The least I could do was keep an open mind. As for Nick and Beej—if they ended up together, well, maybe that was meant to be. Maybe Nick was right about us. Maybe we were too different from each other. But that didn't mean I didn't care.

. . .

"... Mars ...," Ben said. At least, that's what I heard.

"Mars?" I said.

Ben gave me a look. "March—not Mars. You're not even listening."

"I'm sorry. I was thinking about something else."

"It sounds like that project you and Morgan are working on is taking over your brain. Or is there something else on your mind?"

"My teachers are really piling on the homework," I said. "I guess I'm just feeling pressured. What were you saying?"

I felt bad lying to him, but it would have been worse if I'd told him the truth. A guy who considers himself your boyfriend does not want to know that while you're with him, you're thinking about another guy—especially an ex-boyfriend. But that's what I had been doing.

"I was saying that we should start making plans for March. One more week of school, and we're sprung for a whole week."

Originally, we were supposed to spend spring break at his family's cabin with Morgan and Billy. Morgan had been looking forward to it—especially after she heard that he had a hot tub. But a massive storm at the end of February had toppled a lot of trees up north. Two enormous ones had fallen on Ben's family's place. So we were city-bound.

"We could do some day trips," Ben said. "Cross-country skiing—or downhill, if you like—hiking . . . What do you say?"

My cell phone trilled. I checked the display: "Schuster, M." It couldn't be Mr. Schuster. I guessed Isobel. I was right.

"Can you come over here tomorrow?" she said.

"What for?"

"My dad wants to meet you."

"He does?"

"Grandpa really enjoyed your visit," she said. "I suggested that my dad hire you to walk Orion. Grandpa liked the idea. But my dad wants to check you out."

"What do you mean?"

"He's like that. He ran a check on Nick."

"He did?"

"That's how he found out that he'd been in trouble with the police. That's why he fired him. You haven't been in any trouble, have you, Robyn?"

I thought about a nasty little accident that had occurred during one of Billy's animal rights demonstrations last summer. I ended up under arrest, but my mom managed to get the charges dropped—in exchange for my doing community service at the animal shelter where I'd met Nick and Mr. Schuster.

"Nothing your dad would worry about," I told Isobel. I didn't tell her that I wasn't sure I wanted the job.

"There's just one thing," she said. "It's probably not a good idea to tell my dad that you know Nick. In fact, it's probably not a good idea to mention it to anyone in my family. If Dad thinks you know Nick, he won't hire you. Okay?"

I hesitated. A picture forming in my mind, one that explained how Nick had ended up in so much trouble:

Mr. Schuster has a stroke. When his family shows up at the house—surprise!—they find Nick camped out on the couch. They talk to Mr. Schuster, though, and at first they go along with his wishes. Elliot hires Nick to look after Orion. But when he finds out about Nick's record, he does what a lot of people would do in his position— he fires Nick, cutting him off from his beloved Orion.

To the rest of the world, this might seem under-standable. But it wouldn't be understandable to Nick. What if he'd reacted the way he'd done so many times in the past? What if he flew into a rage? What if he really did take those coins, because he was lashing out? What if he'd gone back to the house afterward to explain and had ended up lashing out again, at Mr. Schuster's daughter-in-law? But then why had he asked me to tell Mr. Schuster that he hadn't done it? Was he too ashamed to tell the truth? That would explain why he wasn't doing anything to help himself. He was ready to take whatever punishment some judge would give him.

I could see Nick's aunt and Glen believing that was what had happened. I could see the cops believing it. I could see Elliot Schuster believing it. But after my brief visit today, I couldn't see Mr. Schuster believing it—not the stealing part, anyway.

Suppose Nick hadn't stolen those coins? Suppose he'd been falsely accused and had wanted to explain that to Mr. Schuster, but Claudia Schuster had blocked him? Maybe he'd tried to get past her and things had got out of hand. That didn't excuse the assault, but it did explain it. It also meant that no matter what, Nick was in trouble.

"Robyn?" Isobel said. "Is it okay? Can you come over?"

"Okay," I said. "I'll be there tomorrow after school."

"Be where?" Ben said after I'd finished the call and dropped my cell phone into my backpack.

"A friend of the family had a stroke," I said. "I offered to help around the house."

"I'll go with you if you want," Ben said. "Two can get twice as much done as one."

That was Ben. Kind, considerate, always ready to lend a hand—all the qualities that had attracted me to him in the first place. And how was I repaying him?

By lying to him, that's how.

CHAPTER **SIX**

A tall, thin man answered Mr. Schuster's door the next afternoon. He had the same long nose as Mr. Schuster and the same hazel eyes.

"You must be Robyn," he said. "I'm Elliot Schuster. Come in."

He hung up my coat while I pulled off my boots.

"Let's go in here." He gestured to Mr. Schuster's den. "Forgive the mess." A laptop computer sat open on the desk. Every available surface was piled high with paper. "I'm basically running my business from here until we see what sort of recovery my father is going to make. Please, have a seat."

I sat down in a chair facing the desk.

"Isobel tells me that you know my father from the animal shelter," Elliot said.

"That's right. I met him last summer when I volunteered there."

"She also tells me that you're acquainted with that beast of his."

"I know Orion looks scary," I said. "But he's actually well-behaved." For Nick, at least.

"Try telling that to my wife. He bit her the day we arrived, and since then he's done nothing but bark and growl. The children are terrified of him. I don't know why my father would adopt such a creature." He shook his head in bewilderment. "But he feels strongly about the animal, and I'm not inclined to jeopardize his recovery by getting rid of the dog—unless I'm forced to. Isobel says you're good with him?"

"Well, I—"

"I need someone to walk him. I could hire a professional walker, but they usually take charge of half a dozen or more dogs at a time. My father's needs are more specific. He wants to be able to visit with his dog. He's making a good physical recovery, but he isn't strong enough to handle it on his own and he can't give it voice commands. To be honest, I'm not even sure how well my father understands what's going on."

I was surprised to hear him say that. Mr. Schuster had seemed to understand everything when I had visited.

"In any case, I can't have that animal running free in the house," he continued. "I need someone who can control him while he's with my father. I would pay you for your time, of course."

I had thought about my answer all night. I'd seen how grateful Mr. Schuster was to see Orion and how thrilled poor Orion had been to finally get out of the basement and visit his master. And looking after Orion would give me a chance to try to figure out exactly what had happened. I handed Elliot an envelope.

"What's this?" he said.

"Isobel told me why you wanted to see me, so I put together a résumé," I said.

He opened the envelope and unfolded the sheets of paper inside. The first contained my name, address, and phone number; the academic awards I had won; the volunteering I had done—anything I could think of that would show him how reliable and responsible I was. On the second sheet were my parents' names, occupations, and phone numbers, and the names of some people who could say something nice about me: a teacher, my school principal, and Morgan's parents. Elliot looked impressed.

"After you talk to my references, if you want to hire me, I can start tomorrow," I said.

"Actually, I was hoping you could start right now," he said. "That dog hasn't been walked in days. Even I feel sorry for it."

. . .

There was a boy in the front hall when I emerged from Mr. Schuster's den. He looked eerily like Isobel. He even seemed to be the same age. He regarded me with keen interest.

"Connor, this is Robyn," Elliot Schuster said. "I've just hired her to walk Grandpa's dog." To me, he said, "Connor is my son. He and Isobel are twins."

I said hello. Connor murmured a greeting in response. But when he saw me head for the basement door, he retreated into the living room and closed the French doors behind him. He was still there when I brought Orion up from the basement. I held tightly to Orion's leash, unsure how he would react in the presence of two clearly nervous people.

"Sit," I told the big dog. Instead of obeying me instantly, the way he had the day before, he started to bark.

"Orion, sit," I said again. He kept right on barking. My cheeks burned. Isobel had told her father that I could handle Orion. I didn't want him to think I couldn't. I tried to remember what Nick did whenever Orion became too excited to pay attention. I gripped the leash closer to Orion's collar. "Sit," I said again, in a firmer tone this time.

Mercifully, it worked. Orion dropped his rear end to the floor.

"Good boy," I said. I was so grateful that I felt like hugging him. "Stay," I said. I wound the leash around my wrist. Connor watched me from the other side of the glass doors. Elliot backed up a few paces. But Orion sat quietly and watched me pull on my boots.

"Connor," Elliot called to his son. "Go and get the dog's booties."

"Booties?" I said.

"My father takes good care of his animals," Elliot said. "He always has. The booties protect the dog's paws from all the salt they throw on the sidewalks." He looked at Connor, who hadn't moved. "Get a plastic bag too. There are some under the sink."

"Why can't she get it herself?" Connor said, his voice muffled by the closed doors. "You're paying her, aren't you?"

"*Now*, Connor."

Connor opened the doors slowly, as if he were afraid that any sudden move would set Orion off.

"For heaven's sake," Elliot said. "Robyn has a good grip on the dog. There's nothing to be afraid of."

Connor didn't take his eyes off Orion for even a second as he inched out of the living room and ducked into the kitchen. He appeared in the doorway a few moments later and tossed me four dog booties and a balled-up plastic bag.

"You can clean up the basement while the dog is out," Elliot told him.

Connor looked stricken at the thought. "But that dog's been down there for days . . ."

Yuck. I was glad I didn't have to tackle that job.

"Exactly," Elliot said. "It's about time someone cleaned up the mess."

"Aw, Dad—"

"Never mind the 'Aw, Dad.' Just do it, Connor."

Orion must have known that the booties meant he was going for a walk because he offered his paws one by one so that I could put them on him. Elliot seemed impressed.

"You really do handle him well," he said.

Orion was being so good that I started to feel almost cocky. Big mistake. The instant I opened the door, he dove through. I held fast to his leash as he dragged me across the porch, down the steps, and onto the front walk. For the first time in weeks, it started to snow.

Orion was reasonably well behaved on our outing. He stopped once to do what dogs do when they get outside. I held my breath, closed my eyes, used the plastic bag to pick up after him, and added another item to the long list of reasons I didn't want a dog of my own. I nearly suffered a dislocated shoulder when Orion spotted a squirrel and darted off after it. We stayed out for an hour. The snow kept coming down.

On the way back to Mr. Schuster's house, we passed some of his neighbors out shoveling their driveways. A few of them smiled when they saw the big black dog trot by. Two women crossed the street to greet him. It was obvious that Orion knew them because he didn't bark or growl.

"Good boy," one of the women said. She was the taller of the two and had lively blue eyes. She scratched Orion behind one ear, which set his tail twitching. "You handle him well," she said.

"Are you Mort's granddaughter?" the other woman said. She was shorter and stouter, with sharp brown eyes.

"No. I'm just a friend." When she looked surprised, I explained how I knew Mr. Schuster.

"Ah," the first woman said. "A fellow animal lover. Well, it's good to see Orion out and about again. We were worried, weren't we, Esther?" The shorter woman nodded. "We haven't seen him in ages, and we know that Mort's son isn't fond of dogs."

"How is Mort?" Esther said. "We've dropped by the house a couple of times, but they never let us in to see him. They keep telling us he's sleeping."

I gave them an update on his condition. "He's lucky his son is here to look after him," I added.

Esther did not look impressed. "I've lived across the street from Mort for twenty-five years," she said. "I used to play bridge with Ruth, his wife. But I can count on one hand the number of times Elliot came to visit when Ruth was ill. Since then?" She shook her head. "You'd think he lived on the other side of the world."

"Now, Esther," the taller woman said. "It's not our place to judge."

"I'm not judging," Esther said. "I'm just stating a fact. Elliot Schuster was properly raised. But some children are just plain selfish. They think their parents are only there to bail them out whenever they get into trouble."

What was she talking about? Was she saying that Elliot had been in some kind of trouble?

"I don't think that's fair, Esther," the taller woman murmured.

"It's perfectly fair, Edith," Esther said. "You know as well as I do that that boy never came to visit unless he needed money. And when he did, he always asked Ruth, never Mort, because he knew Ruth would never say no to him." She turned to me. "Mort told me himself that there comes a time when a child has to stand on his own two feet. But Ruth never denied Elliot anything."

"He was her only child," Edith said.

"And how did he repay her?" Esther retorted "He didn't even show up for her funeral. Told his father he couldn't get away. And have you seen him around here since then?"

"Well, he's here now, and that's the important thing," Edith said.

"He probably only came for the same reason he showed up when Ruth was ill—to make sure that he's in his father's will." Esther sniffed. "If I were Mort, I'd leave all my money to charity." No wonder Elliot didn't ask her into the house. "He's making a real show of it too. The whole family is camped out over there. If he thinks that's going to impress anyone, he can think again. And what about those children of his? Shouldn't they be in school?"

Edith smiled weakly at me. "We really should let you go, dear," she said.

But Esther had more to say.

"I heard there was a break-in at Mort's place," she said. "The police came around with pictures, asking if we'd seen anyone lurking around the house. Do you know anything about that?"

I shook my head. What pictures? Pictures of Nick?

"It had something to do with that boy who used to walk Orion for Mort," Esther said. "Gene McGrath told me he heard he was a criminal. Can you imagine?"

"Mort wouldn't have hired him if he was a criminal, Esther."

"Gene said that's the reason Elliot sent the boy packing—he found out he had a police record."

"I thought he seemed very nice," Edith said. "He was always polite. And he certainly seemed fond of Orion."

"Well, when the police asked me if I'd seen anyone around who looked like they were up to no good, I told them, 'You bet I did.' I said I'd seen that boy skulking about after Elliot fired him. On the day they mentioned too."

Terrific, I thought. At least one of Mr. Schuster's neighbors had identified Nick as a troublemaker.

Esther's sharp eyes searched mine. "Did they tell you if anything was stolen?"

I was pretty sure that anything I told Esther would make its way quickly around the neighborhood, so I shook my head.

"I should be going," I said. "When I see Mr. Schuster, I'll tell him that you were asking about him."

"Please do," Edith said. "Tell him Esther and Edith wish him well and that if there's anything we can do—anything at all—he has only to call."

Orion and I were halfway up Mr. Schuster's driveway when a car pulled up alongside of us. A tall, burly man in a gray overcoat climbed out of it. Orion strained against the leash, barking and growling. It took all my strength to hold him. The man held up his hands in mock surrender.

"Friend, not foe," he said.

"Orion, quiet," I said. But Orion continued to bark. His tail was straight out. So were his ears. I wondered if he and the man had met before.

"That's a fierce-looking dog," the man said. He smiled, but the look in his eyes didn't match the expression on his face. "Is your mother here?"

"I don't know," I said. "Mr. Schuster—Elliot Schuster—is home, but I don't live here. I'm just the dog walker. Do you want me to tell him you're here?"

"That would be great, thanks," the man said. He watched Orion and me go onto the porch, but he didn't follow us. I think he wanted to keep his distance. Orion had that effect on people.

I opened the door and called Elliot. He strode out of the den, holding the list of references I had given him.

"Ah, Robyn," he said. "I called your school and spoke to your principal. She had nothing but good things to say about you. As far as I'm concerned, you've got the job. Welcome aboard."

"Thank you," I said. "There's a man outside to see you."

"Finally," Elliot exclaimed. He headed for the door. Orion must have seen the opportunity for another walk because he charged after him, nearly dislocating my shoulder. Elliot froze.

"Orion, sit," I said sternly. To my immense relief, he obeyed. "Sorry," I said to Elliot. "He loves to be outside."

Elliot nodded tersely. He steered a wide path around us and stepped outside. Through the screen door, I heard Elliot say, "Are you from the insurance company? I must say, I haven't been impressed by the service—"

"I'm not from the insurance company," the man said. "I was hoping to speak to Mrs. Schuster. Is she here?"

"No, she isn't."

"Do you expect her back soon?"

"I'm not sure when she'll be back," Elliot said.

"Would you please tell her that Mr. Jones dropped by," the man said, "and that I'll be in touch?"

"Can I tell her what this is about?" Elliot said.

"She'll know," Mr. Jones said.

I heard humming behind me and turned toward the sound. Connor was coming out of the kitchen with a can of pop and a bag of potato chips. When he saw Orion, the color drained from his face.

"It's okay," I said. "He won't—"

The front door opened, and Elliot came back inside, muttering to himself. It was too much activity for Orion. He leapt to his feet and started barking. Connor scrambled back into the kitchen. I held fast to Orion's leash and tried to calm him down.

"Would you like me to take him upstairs to see your father?" I said.

Elliot shook his head.

"The physical therapist was here while you were out. Dad is getting around quite well with a walker now. He's so determined, but I'm afraid all that exertion wears him out. Perhaps tomorrow." He went back into the den, frowning.

As usual, Orion balked at returning to the basement. By the time I had settled him, Connor was outside shoveling the driveway. He paused for a moment and looked at me but didn't say anything. I decided to take the initiative.

"Orion's bark is far worse than his bite," I said, smiling at him.

"Tell that to my mother," Connor said grimly.

"He was probably just startled," I said. "He's a great dog. Really. Ask your grandfather."

"I don't like dogs."

"I didn't used to like them, either," I said. "I was bitten once when I was a kid. I was terrified of dogs after that."

"You don't look scared now."

"That's because I learned more about dogs from your grandfather." I'd learned even more from Nick, but I wasn't going to tell him that.

"My dad says you volunteer at the animal shelter where Grandpa used to volunteer."

"I volunteered there last summer. That's where I met your grandfather," I said.

"Do you know a guy named Nick?"

Isobel had warned me not to let anyone in her family know that Nick and I were even acquainted.

"No," I said. "Why?"

"My grandfather said he met a guy named Nick at the animal shelter. If you volunteered there, you must know him."

"There are a lot of volunteers at the shelter," I said. "I mainly met the ones who worked in the office. That's where I did most of my volunteering. What does this Nick do at the shelter?"

"My grandfather said he was in some kind of special dog-training program."

"I didn't have anything to do with the dog training."

"So you don't know Nick? He didn't send you here?"

It sounded like Nick had made as negative an impression on Connor as he had on Elliot.

"I heard your grandfather was sick, so I came to see how he was doing," I said. "That's all."

"How did you hear?" he said. "Who told you?"

"Someone at the animal shelter," I said. It was the only answer I could think of that might satisfy him.

Connor studied me for a moment as if I were a puzzle he was trying to solve.

A car horn tooted. Connor and I stepped aside to let a dark blue Honda into the driveway. Isobel got out of the passenger side. She smiled and waved to me.

"Did you get the job?" she said.

I nodded.

A woman climbed out of the driver's side. Isobel introduced me.

"Mom, this is Robyn, the girl Daddy hired to walk Grandpa's dog."

Claudia Schuster nodded shyly at me and said she was pleased to meet me. She confessed that she wasn't much of a dog person but that she could see that Orion was important to her father-in-law and that she was glad I would be looking after him until they made more permanent arrangements. I wondered what she meant by that. Just as I was about to leave, Elliot came to the door and called to his wife: "A Mr. Jones came by to see you. He said he'd drop by again. Who is he, Claudia?"

There was a moment's pause before she said, "He must be from the home care service I called. We can't stay here forever, Elliot. And your dad is going to need some help after we leave."

I found it hard to believe that Mr. Jones, with his phony smile, could be in the business of helping people. But you never know.

On the way home, I called Nick's aunt's house. I'd decided that I should at least put Nick's mind to rest and tell him that I'd seen Orion.

Glen answered the phone. When I asked if I could speak with Nick, he said, "No, you may not. And stop calling here. Nick is not allowed to come to the phone."

"But—"

He hung up on me.

What did he mean, stop calling? It was the first time I had tried.

CHAPTER **SEVEN**

I felt so sorry for Orion that I got up extra early the next morning to take him for a short walk before school. The minute classes were over that afternoon, I ran to get my backpack so I could take him for a longer walk. He was a big dog and needed plenty of exercise. Morgan was waiting for me at my locker.

"Um, excuse me, but weren't we planning to work on our project?" she said. "Or have you decided to delegate all of the work to me?"

"I have to walk Orion," I said as I slung my backpack over my shoulder. "Come over to my dad's place after supper. We'll work on it then. I promise."

. . .

Elliot answered the door at Mr. Schuster's house.

"Robyn, hi," he said. "I have someone here, so I can't

chat. The physical therapist just left. Why don't you take the dog upstairs before you walk him, while Dad is still awake?"

He went into the living room. As I hung up my coat, I couldn't help but overhear part of his conversation.

"I had those coins insured so that if anything were to happen to them, my father would be compensated," Elliot was saying. "Now something has happened. They've been stolen. I filed a claim on my father's behalf. I don't understand what the delay is."

I went to the basement to get Orion. He barked when he heard me on the stairs, but he stopped when I got to the bottom and jumped up so that his front paws were on the barrier. He wagged his tail when he saw me reach for his leash. I clipped it onto his collar and slid the barrier aside so that he could pass.

"Perhaps, Mr. Schuster, I should speak with your father," another man was saying when Orion and I emerged from the basement.

"My father isn't able to communicate verbally at this point," Elliot said. "We're not even sure how much he really understands. While he's ill, I'm in charge of his affairs, and I demand to know why this is taking so long."

"Your father's coin collection is extremely valuable, as I'm sure you know," the other man said. "Before we settle the claim, we have an obligation to make sure that the coins are unrecoverable or that they weren't misplaced. If I could just ask you a few more questions . . ."

I guided Orion to the stairs.

"Misplaced?" Elliot said. "The side door to the house was pried open with a crowbar. The coins are gone. The police made an arrest."

Orion and I climbed the stairs.

"I've read the police report, Mr. Schuster," the man from the insurance company said. His voice was soft, almost soothing. "But you arranged for that policy only recently—"

As soon as we got to the top of the stairs, Orion bolted into Mr. Schuster's room, dragging me with him. We almost knocked over the walker that was standing just inside the door and startled Isobel, who was sitting beside Mr. Schuster, and her mother, who was straightening the sheets on the bed. They both stared fearfully at Orion. I shortened the leash to keep him close to me. Only Mr. Schuster smiled. I glanced at Isobel.

"Remember what I showed you?" I said.

She hesitated and then nodded. She got up and crept toward Orion, one hand extended, watching him warily in case she had to snap her hand away from his enormous teeth.

"Isobel, be careful," Claudia Schuster said, her voice shrill with anxiety.

"Don't worry," I said, trying to reassure her so that the fear in her voice wouldn't set Orion off. "If you relax, Isobel, he'll relax."

Isobel drew in a deep breath and slowly exhaled. She let Orion sniff her hand. Slowly, cautiously, she ran a hand over the top of his head and scratched behind the big dog's ear. His tail began to flick merrily back and forth. Isobel looked at me and smiled.

"See?" I said. "He looks like a big, mean old dog, but he's really a pussycat."

I led Orion—okay, so he led me—to the chair where Mr. Schuster was sitting so that he could pat him. Orion roowfed softly.

"He misses you, Mr. Schuster," I said.

"I told Grandpa that Daddy hired you to walk him," Isobel said. "He's happy about that, aren't you, Grandpa?"

Mr. Schuster nodded.

"The physical therapist said Grandpa's making great progress. Didn't he, Mom?"

Claudia Schuster nodded as she hastily finished making the bed. She seemed to be in a hurry to get out of the room.

I heard footsteps on the stairs. Mr. Schuster turned toward the door. His lopsided smile disappeared when he saw Elliot.

"Well?" Claudia said.

Elliot sighed. He turned to Mr. Schuster. "I just spoke to the insurance adjuster, Dad. He says it's going to take time before they settle the claim and pay you for the loss of your coin collection."

"Time?" Claudia said. "How much time?"

"He didn't say. But you know how insurance companies are. Sometimes I think they'll do anything to weasel out of paying up."

"Do you think they're trying to weasel out of this claim?" Claudia said.

"Apparently the problem is that they were just recently insured. Too recently, according to the insurance adjuster. And the fact that you employed that boy, knowing what you did about him—" He shook his head in exasperation. "It seems that they're not fully satisfied with the facts of the case. He kept asking me if I was sure there wasn't any way the coins might have gone astray."

"Gone astray?" Claudia said.

"He didn't come right out and say it, but I don't think he's convinced that the coins were stolen."

"I don't understand," Claudia said. "The police arrested that boy. They're sure he did it. They even found some of the coins—"

"The way he was talking, I got the impression that the insurance company suspects us of having staged the robbery so that we could collect the insurance money," Elliot said.

"Why would we do that?" Isobel said. "Everyone knows how much Grandpa loves his coin collection. He loves it almost as much as he loves Orion."

Elliot stepped tentatively into the room. Orion sprang to his feet and barked. There was nothing aggressive about his stance, but Elliot immediately retreated.

"I'm sorry, Dad," he said. "I thought that insuring your collection would protect you if anything happened. It appears that I might have been mistaken. The insurance adjuster says he'll keep me posted."

Claudia edged around Orion and followed her husband down the stairs. I stayed a little longer so that Mr. Schuster could visit with Orion. I watched as he scratched Orion affectionately and the dog licked his hand. I hated to take Orion away, but he needed his walk.

"I'll bring him back to see you tomorrow," I said.

"Can I walk him with you?" Isobel asked.

"If you want to."

She looked at her grandfather. "Do you mind, Grandpa? Maybe I can get to know Orion as well as Robyn does. Then maybe I can look after him for you."

The old man beamed crookedly at her. She bent down and kissed him on the cheek before following Orion and me downstairs.

Isobel was braver than I had expected. She even tried to help me with Orion's booties, until one of his nails got caught on the fastenings and he yelped. She jumped back, startled.

"It's okay," I said. "I've done that myself a couple of times. He's fine."

But she stood at a distance and waited while I secured the rest of the booties.

"Do you want to hold the leash?" I asked Isobel.

She looked warily at the big dog but finally extended her hand. I gave her the leash, and she wound it around her wrist as she had seen me do.

"The only thing you have to worry about is if he sees a—"

Roowf-roowf! Orion was off like a shot, yanking Isobel almost off her feet.

"—squirrel," I said.

Isobel scrambled after Orion, her arm extended out straight in front of her. I raced after her, calling for Orion to stay and sit. He didn't listen. He didn't stop galloping, either, until the frightened squirrel had taken refuge up a maple tree. Orion stood at the bottom of the tree, barking excitedly as if he thought it would encourage the squirrel to come back down and play some more.

"Orion, sit," I said again, more firmly this time.

He kept barking.

"Orion! Sit!"

The big dog plunked his rear end down into the snow, but I think that was only because the squirrel had vanished from sight. After he had calmed down, we continued our walk. When Orion couldn't find any more squirrels, he seemed content to trot along at Isobel's side. I kept pace with her. She relaxed a little.

"You're right," she said. "He's not so bad once you get to know him."

"Now if you could just convince the rest of your family."

Isobel looked doubtful. "My dad may change his mind, but there's no way my mom or Connor will. Especially not Connor."

"Because Orion bit your mom?"

"Connor was attacked by a dog—a Rottweiler— when he was nine," Isobel said. "Came out of nowhere and dragged him off his bicycle. It took three guys to get the dog off him. Connor was in the hospital for a week. You should see the scars on his leg."

I knew how he felt. I'd been afraid of dogs too as a result of being bitten. But a nip on my bottom was nothing compared to an all-out attack.

"They put the dog down," Isobel added. "Ever since then, Connor has insisted that he hates dogs, but really he's afraid of them, especially big ones like Orion. That's why I'm worried about what will happen to Orion if Grandpa doesn't get better. Mom still wants Dad to hand him over to an animal shelter. But Dad says he wants to wait and see how well Grandpa recovers."

We walked for a few moments in silence, Orion trotting along happily beside us, pulling on his leash now and then so that he could sniff yellow patches in the snow.

"I wish we visited Grandpa more often," Isobel said with a sigh. "I feel bad about seeing him only now that he's sick."

"When was the last time you were here?"

"Maybe three years ago? Before Grandma died."

"You haven't seen your grandfather in three years? Is that why the whole family came instead of just your father?"

She shook her head. "My mom offered to come by herself to look after Grandpa. My dad has his own business, so it's hard for him to get away. But Dad said no. He said Grandpa is his father, so he should come too."

"What about you and Connor? Aren't you missing school?"

"Mom made arrangements with our principal. We get our assignments by e-mail, and Mom is making sure we keep up. She says she's glad we all came. I think she feels bad about what happened when Grandma died."

"What do you mean?"

"Mom and Dad were away on a trip for my dad's business. My dad wanted to go to the funeral, but he just couldn't. Grandpa got really mad. When Grandma was alive, she and Grandpa used to phone us every Sunday. But after Grandma died, Grandpa stopped calling. He keeps in touch with Connor and me, but he and my dad hardly speak to each other."

"You seem to have a good relationship with him," I said.

She smiled. "He e-mails me almost every day and tells me about what he's been doing and who he meets. And he and Connor are always e-mailing each other about coin auctions and shows. Connor is as crazy about coins as Grandpa."

"And you're not?"

She shook her head. "I don't find them as fascinating as he and Connor do. I didn't understand what the big deal was until one night when my dad said he'd heard about a coin that had sold for thousands of dollars. He said it was too bad that Grandpa didn't have any like that. You should have seen the look on his face when Connor told him that Grandpa had a couple of them— and a lot of others that were worth even more."

"I guess the whole collection must have been pretty valuable," I said.

"So valuable that when my dad found out that Grandpa had promised to leave the whole thing to Connor, he freaked. He said a collection like that was far too much to leave to one person and that it should go to the whole family. Connor didn't like that. He's the only one besides Grandpa who knows anything about coins. He says he loves them because of their history, not because of what they're worth. I think he was more upset than anyone else when they were stolen."

No wonder Connor had grilled me about Nick. Mr. Schuster's coin collection was supposed to be Connor's one day.

"Did your parents suspect Nick right away?"

"I'm not sure. But when the police came, they asked if there was anyone besides the family who knew that Grandpa had a coin collection, knew where he kept it."

"Where did he keep it? In a safe or locked up somewhere?"

She shook her head. "In the back bedroom—the one my parents are using now. The police also asked if anyone else had been in the house. That's when my dad told them about Nick. He said that he'd fired Nick but that Nick had kept coming around."

"He did?"

"The first time he came, he and my dad got into an argument. Nick wanted to see Orion. He tried to tell

Dad that he'd changed. He said there were people Dad could talk to, if he didn't believe him."

"Your dad didn't go for it, huh?"

"He threatened to call the police if Nick didn't leave."

"And Nick came back again after that?"

"That's what my dad said. He told the police that he wouldn't be surprised if Nick had a grudge. Then Connor told them that Nick knew exactly how much the coins were worth."

I could just imagine how the police had reacted to that information.

"How did Connor know that?" I said.

"Grandpa e-mailed him about Nick. He said he was teaching Nick all about coins."

One more reason for the police to be suspicious.

"When my dad heard that, he got really mad. He said Grandpa had been foolish to let Nick in the house. He said that once Nick knew how valuable the coins were, of course he would want to steal them. I guess the police must have thought so too. My dad said that because Nick is a youth, probably the most he'll get is two years. Dad's really mad about that. He says it's not nearly enough."

I wanted to spring to Nick's defense, but without any facts to back me up . . .

"Robyn, why are you so interested in Nick?"

"We're . . . friends."

"You used to be more than that, didn't you?" Isobel said. She smiled gently. "When I saw that picture of you and he said you were just someone he knew, I knew there was more to it than that. I could tell by the way he said it."

"We used to go out," I admitted. "But that's over."

She looked at me as if she didn't believe me. But she didn't say anything else about Nick.

We walked home in silence. I don't know what Isobel was thinking about, but my mind was on Nick. Two years may have seemed like nothing to Elliot, but to Nick, it would sound like a lifetime. He'd been doing so well lately. He'd worked hard at getting his life on track. What would he be like after two years in jail, especially if it was for something he hadn't done? Would he ever get over the anger he'd feel? Would he ever be able to get back to a normal life? Would he even want to?

CHAPTER **EIGHT**

Morgan came over after supper, and we settled at my dad's enormous dining table to work on our project. Morgan seemed to be making good progress, but I was just going through the motions. I couldn't get Nick out of my mind. After a while, my dad brought us tea and cookies.

"Okay, that makes it an official time-out," Morgan said. She reached for a cookie. "How's the dog walking going?"

My father glanced at me on his way back to the kitchen, but he didn't say anything.

"It's okay," I said.

"Have you found out anything?"

"Just that poor Orion spends most of his time locked in the basement. And that it doesn't look good for Nick. Everyone is convinced that he stole Mr. Schuster's coin collection."

"Everyone?" she said. "Does that include you?"

I gave her a sharp look.

"I didn't think so," she said. She took another sip of tea. "Have you talked to him again?"

"I tried calling, but Glen wouldn't let him come to the phone."

"So now what?"

"That coin collection didn't just walk away," I said. "Someone took it."

"Obviously," Morgan said. "But who?"

I'd been thinking about that too. But even if I was on the right track, how was I going to prove it?

"I'm working on it," I said.

"What about Ben?"

"What about him?"

"Does he know what you're up to?"

"Not exactly."

"Not exactly?"

"Okay. No, he doesn't know."

"Does he know that Nick is back in town?"

I shook my head.

Morgan didn't say anything as she took another nibble of the cookie, but sometimes silence is louder than words.

"Come on, Morgan. You saw how Nick acted when we were there. He's not interested in me anymore."

"Nick saw you with Ben. If Billy's right, he saw you take off the necklace he sent you and put on Ben's ring instead. Maybe he acted the way he did because you broke his heart."

"Well, if I did, he broke mine first. He's the one who walked out on me."

"You didn't even ask him why he did it."

"What's the matter with you?" I said. "You were the one who kept telling me to forget about him. You told me Ben was the perfect guy for me. Over and over." I couldn't believe how angry I was. I stared down at the table and took a couple of deep breaths to try to calm down.

"I'm sorry," Morgan said quietly. "I should have kept my mouth shut. But you were such a mess after Nick left. I just wanted you to be happy. I just want you to be happy now."

"In that case," I said, "we should get back to work."

.   .   .

It was late by the time we finished, so my father offered to drive Morgan home. When he got back, I was still sitting at the dining table. My laptop was open in front of me, but I hadn't looked at it the whole time he was gone. Instead, I'd been staring up at the moon through the raised skylight in the ceiling over the table. I'd been thinking about Nick.

"What's this about walking a dog?" my father said after he'd hung up his coat.

"I got a job as a dog walker."

That earned me a raised eyebrow. "I thought you didn't like dogs."

"I'm doing it as a special favor."

"Really? Whose dog are you walking?"

I hesitated. "Mr. Schuster's."

"I see." My dad sat down at the table opposite me. His expression was somber. "Nick really got himself jammed up this time, Robbie."

I swallowed hard. He wouldn't be saying that if he didn't know something.

"Who did you talk to?"

"I know one of the arresting officers."

I was afraid to ask: "And?"

"And, on the night in question, Mr. Schuster's family went out to dinner." He dug into a pocket, pulled out the notebook he always carried, and thumbed through it. "They left the house at seven thirty. When they returned a little after nine thirty, Claudia Schuster went into the kitchen and noticed that the kitchen window was open a few inches. She swore it had been closed when she left the house."

"I thought the thief came in through the side door."

"He did," my father said. "The theory is that he tried the kitchen window first. The screen was already loose. But according to Mr. Schuster, that window has been broken for years. It only opens about six inches. No way anyone could have got in that way. Then Elliot Schuster went down to the basement to check on Mr. Schuster's dog and noticed something amiss with the side door. The lock was broken. Pried open."

"With a crowbar," I said.

Dad nodded. "The family also discovered that Mr. Schuster's coins were gone. As far as they could tell, it was the only thing missing. They called the police. During the investigation, Nick's name came up. When the police finally tracked him down, they found some of the stolen coins in his backpack, together with a thousand in cash."

Nobody had mentioned that. "Where did Nick get a thousand dollars?"

My father did not look happy. "Apparently he declined to explain."

That didn't sound good. It didn't sound good at all.

"There's more, Robbie. They also found the crowbar that was used to pry open the door. And Nick was seen in the area earlier that day."

I already knew that. Esther had told me.

"He was probably just trying to make sure that Orion was okay," I said. "He loves that dog, Dad."

"Nick has no alibi for when it happened, Robbie," Dad said softly. "He can't account for his whereabouts. They've offered to reduce or even drop some of the charges if he tells them what he did with the rest of the coins, but he isn't cooperating."

"But did he confess? Did he admit he did it?"

My dad shook his head. "He maintains he doesn't know anything about it."

"You don't really think he did it, do you?"

"I haven't talked to him, Robbie, so I have no basis to form an opinion. I'd like to think that he didn't. But based on what the arresting officer told me, if this were my case? I would have arrested Nick too and I'd feel sure I had the right person."

I'd been hoping my father would answer differently. I wanted someone—someone besides Beej—to believe in Nick's innocence. I wanted someone to tell me that I was right to believe in him.

"Mr. Schuster's coin collection was insured, Dad. But when I was there today visiting Mr. Schuster, his son said that the insurance company was asking a lot of questions because they had been insured only recently. Why does that matter?"

"It depends. How recent is recent?" my father said.

"I don't know. What difference does it make?"

"Has Mr. Schuster had his collection for a long time?"

"His granddaughter told me that he's been collecting for years."

"I see."

"See what?"

"Okay, example one: A person has a valuable coin collection. Has had it insured for, say, ten years. He pays the premiums every year and nothing happens to the coins. Then, after ten years, his house is broken into and the coins are stolen. He calls the police and they make an arrest. In that case, the owner of the coins probably wouldn't have any trouble collecting from the insurance company."

"I still don't—"

"Example two," my father said. "The same person has the same valuable coin collection but hasn't had it insured the whole time it's been in his possession. Suddenly he decides to buy a policy. One month later, he reports that the collection has been stolen. He tells the police that he thinks it was taken by a boy who worked for him, who he knew had a criminal record.

"In that case," my father continued, "the insurance company might be justifiably suspicious. They might think that the person took out the policy because he *planned* to make a claim."

"You mean that he was planning to report the coins stolen when they really hadn't been stolen?"

My father nodded.

"But Mr. Schuster's house really was broken into. And the police made an arrest. Why wouldn't the insurance company believe the police?" I was wondering—hoping—that the company's doubts might mean something, something that could help Nick.

"I'm sure they do believe the police, up to a point," my dad said. "There's no doubt that Nick was caught with stolen property. But the police found only a few coins in Nick's backpack. And according to my source, they were the least valuable coins in the collection."

"So . . ?" I said.

"So victims of theft sometimes try to take advantage of the situation. For example, say a person leaves his phone in his car. Someone breaks a window and steals it. The person calls the police and reports the theft. But he tells the police that there was also a brand-new iPad in the car or maybe an expensive camera. After all, who's going to know? He thinks, I've been paying insurance premiums for years, why shouldn't I get something back?"

"So the insurance company might think that Nick only took some coins? That Mr. Schuster said he took them all when he really didn't?"

"It wouldn't be the first time," my father said. "There have also been plenty of cases where people pay someone to stage a robbery so that they can collect the insurance money. Hard to imagine that Mr. Schuster would do anything like that, though, especially since he was in the hospital at the time."

"But the coins wouldn't have been insured in the first place if Mr. Schuster's son hadn't talked him into it," I said.

"Schuster's son took the initiative to have the coins insured? And while the son was staying at the house, the coins were stolen?" My father pondered this. "No wonder the insurance company wants to investigate before they pay up. But, Robbie, even if they find out that Mr. Schuster's son lied about what happened to the coins, Nick still has a lot of explaining to do. Not only did he have some coins in his possession—and a large amount of cash that he refuses to account for *and* that crowbar— he's also being less than cooperative. Add an assault charge to that, and he's still in big trouble."

· · ·

Ben called the next morning, just as I was dashing to school. I'd given Orion a longer-than-usual morning walk—I felt so sorry for him, cooped up in that basement all day—and was a couple of minutes away from being late for homeroom. I let the call ring through to my voice mail and promised myself that I would call him back at lunchtime.

Morgan was waiting for me at my locker at noon. She said something that Morgan hardly ever says: "I'm sorry."

"For what?" I said. "You didn't do anything."

"Except harass you to go out with Ben."

"Don't give yourself too much credit," I said. "If I didn't like him, nothing you could have said would have made me go out with him. But I do like him, Morgan. He's really sweet and so considerate. Maybe I don't feel the same way about him as I do about Nick—*did* about Nick. But—I don't feel exactly the same way about you and Billy, but you're both my best friends. Feeling differently isn't necessarily bad, right?"

Morgan said nothing.

"Right, Morgan?"

"I have no opinion," she said firmly, as if trying to convince herself that it was true. "I promised myself that I wouldn't give you any more advice—unless you ask for it."

I laughed. If there was one thing that Morgan lived for—besides shopping—it was dispensing unasked-for advice.

. . .

I went directly to Mr. Schuster's house again after school. My phone rang just as I started up the porch steps. I checked the display. Ben again. I sighed. I really did like him. But . . . Another ring. I pressed the button to answer—and my phone died. I'd forgotten to recharge it. I slipped it back into my pocket and rang the doorbell.

Elliot answered. He had a sheaf of papers in one hand and seemed distracted as he stepped aside to let me enter.

"I'll leave the door unlocked so you can let yourself in after you walk the dog," he said. "You can take him up to see my father when you get back."

There was a telephone on the desk in Mr. Schuster's den and another one sitting on a table in the front hall.

"Would it be okay if I made a quick call?" I said.

"Any time," Elliot said. "You don't even have to ask." He paused as he turned to go back into the den. "Local, right?"

I nodded.

I tried Ben's number and was surprised at my relief when I ended up with his voice mail. I left a message telling him that I wasn't home and that my cell phone battery had died. I promised to call him later.

Orion started barking as soon as I opened the basement door and had his front paws up on the plywood barrier by the time I got to the bottom of the stairs. He couldn't wait to get out of there. I gave him a dog biscuit and attached his leash while he ate it. I couldn't quite believe it, but I was starting to think of him as a canine friend instead of a scary chore. My dad would have been astonished if he'd seen the way I led Orion upstairs and put on his booties.

We walked for an hour. When I let myself back into the house, I saw Mr. Schuster gripping his walker and making his way slowly up the stairs to his room. A big man in a tracksuit was helping him. When they reached the top, the man said, "Congratulations, Mort. You're doing really well. You can go downstairs and have dinner with your family later. But you have to take it slow, okay? And you have to promise you won't go on the stairs alone. You have to have someone to help you."

Mr. Schuster nodded. Isobel beamed at the top of the stairs.

Orion and I followed him into his room. As soon as Mr. Schuster had settled into his armchair, Orion dropped his head onto the old man's lap. Mr. Schuster looked tired but pleased with himself.

"Way to go, Mr. Schuster," I said.

"Tomorrow we're going to celebrate," Isobel said. "My dad is going to the mall to get his hair cut. Grandpa and I are going with him. While my dad's at the barber, we're going to find a nice place to sit and people watch. Right, Grandpa?"

Mr. Schuster smiled lopsidedly at his granddaughter.

When I started back down the stairs with Orion, I saw Connor sprawled on a bed across the hall. When he saw Orion, he shrank back against the wall. I thought about trying to introduce him to the dog the way I had introduced Isobel but decided against it. I understood how he felt. I had felt that way myself—and my experience hadn't been anywhere near as terrifying as his.

I settled Orion back into the basement. As I buttoned my coat afterward in the front hall, I glanced at the phone on the hall table.

Ben.

He had been trying to reach me for hours, and I still hadn't spoken to him. He had to be wondering what was going on. I picked up the phone in the hall to make a quick call—and had the shock of a lifetime.

Nick was on the line.

CHAPTER **NINE**

"The mall," he said. "Noon tomorrow. Upper level, in front of the Gap. I'll be there." I heard a click. He had hung up. I waited until I heard another, slightly louder, click. That told me that whoever he had been talking to had also hung up. Then I gently put down the receiver.

It sounded as if Nick was planning to meet someone at the mall—someone who lived in the house. Isobel had told me that she and Mr. Schuster were going to the mall. Could Nick be planning to meet them? But that would be stupid. One of the conditions of Nick's release was that he had to stay away from Mr. Schuster. Elliot was going to be at the mall too. Could Nick be planning to meet him? But why would he do that? Elliot had fired Nick, had refused to give him a second chance, and had accused him of stealing Mr. Schuster's coins. Then I remembered what my father had told me about insurance claims. I thought about all the cash the police had found when they arrested Nick. I got a sick feeling in my stomach.

Elliot Schuster came out of the den and stopped short when he saw me.

"Robyn," he said, startled. "You're still here."

"I was just on my way home." I crossed quickly to the door, but it swung open before I could grab it. Claudia stepped into the front hall.

"Where have you been all afternoon?" Elliot demanded.

Claudia's cheeks reddened. She glanced at me.

"Well?" Elliot demanded.

"I told you. I had some errands to run."

"What errands? Where? If you—" He broke off when his wife looked at me again. "We'll see you tomorrow then, Robyn," he said.

I took the hint and let myself out. As the door closed behind me, I heard Claudia say, "How could I? You won't let me touch the credit card. You took away my ATM card . . ."

I thought about what Edith and Esther had said about Elliot—and about everything else I had heard about him. I also thought about the insurance policy.

I decided to make a stop on the way home.

.   .   .

Nick's aunt had her overcoat on when she answered the door.

"Robyn," she said, her voice warm and welcoming. "Glen said you came by the other day. How are you?"

"I'm fine, thank you." I hesitated. "Is Nick here?"

"He should be," she said, pulling off her coat. "I just got home." She called Nick's name. He answered with a muffled shout.

"Sounds like he's in the basement," she said.

"Would it be okay if I talked to him for a minute?"

She considered this for a moment before stepping back to let me in.

"I don't know what's going on between you and Nick," she said. "But . . . he's in a lot of trouble this time."

I didn't know what to say, so I just nodded.

I found Nick sitting in the recliner in the basement entertainment room, staring unblinkingly at the TV screen while he flicked through channel after channel.

"Hi, Nick," I said.

He didn't answer. He didn't even look at me. I glanced around the room. There was a phone sitting on one end of the bar. I grabbed the remote from his hand and turned off the TV.

"Don't you want to know how Orion is?" I said.

That got his attention. He turned his purple-blue eyes on me.

"I've seen him," I said. "He's okay."

"They didn't get rid of him?"

"No."

He seemed to relax a little.

"Nick, what are your plans for tomorrow?"

He looked back at the blank TV screen.

"What's it to you?" he said.

"Are you going out?"

"Not that it's any of your business, but, yeah. I have an appointment with my lawyer."

"Is your aunt going with you?"

He straightened up in the recliner and looked at me with irritation.

"She can't. She's working."

"So Glen is going with you?"

"No. I'm going alone."

"Your aunt trusts you to do that?"

"Yeah." He sounded indignant. "Believe it or not, she does. I just have to call her as soon as I get there and before I leave and again when I get home."

That should have made me feel better, but it didn't. If I was right about what Nick was planning, he would have figured out how to make it work.

"Where is your lawyer's office?"

His eyes flashed with anger. "What's with all the questions, Robyn?"

All the way to the house, I had thought about only three things: Nick's voice on the phone, Elliot Schuster, and the $1,000 in cash. Did it all mean what I thought it might?

"Have you talked to Elliot Schuster since you were arrested?"

"What? Why are you asking me that?"

His eyes shifted for a second to the phone on the bar, and my heart sank. I wanted to believe what Beej did—that he hadn't stolen those coins and that anything else he had done was because he felt he'd been treated unfairly. But it was all so confusing. And the cash that the police had found on Nick made it seem so much worse. Did Nick have something to do with the missing coins or not? If he did, what had made him take them?

From what I had heard, both from Isobel and from the neighbors, there was a lot of friction between Elliot and his father. And according to Esther and Edith, Elliot had a history of asking his parents for money. Add to that that he had found out only recently how valuable his father's coin collection was and immediately took out an insurance policy to cover it. Then, shortly after he'd taken up residence in his father's house, the collection had vanished. Maybe there was a good reason for the insurance company to be suspicious. Maybe Elliot had finally figured out a way to get his hands on some money.

What if, after checking Nick out, Elliot had thought a kid with a record would be glad to make some quick cash. Maybe he'd managed to convince Nick to go along with his scheme. Maybe Elliot had even paid him up front, which would explain the money the police had found when they caught up with Nick.

There was just one problem with that theory: I couldn't make myself believe that Nick would ever go along with a scheme to steal from Mr. Schuster.

No, it was more likely he'd do whatever it took to stop Elliot. And what better way to do that than to take the coins himself and hide them somewhere where they would be safe until Mr. Schuster was back on his feet again? That would explain why he had no alibi for the night of the theft, why he tried to see Mr. Schuster as soon as he was released on bail the first time, and why he refused to tell the police where the coins were. There was no way he would want them handed over to Elliot.

Knowing Nick, there was also probably no way he would think the police would believe him if he told them the truth. It would also explain why Nick would go to the mall to meet with Elliot—to confront him or maybe to make some kind of deal with him. Maybe Nick knew what I had sensed so strongly—that Mr. Schuster was reluctant to think the worst of him, even if everyone else did. Maybe Nick thought there was some way he could get the coins back to Mr. Schuster now that he was out of the hospital. Or maybe he was planning to threaten Elliot—if Elliot didn't help him out of the mess he was in, Nick would expose him in court. It was the theory I preferred to believe, even if it turned out I was kidding myself. It didn't explain the coins and the crowbar the police had found, but then, Nick wasn't a thief. Maybe he'd just slipped up. He had probably counted on the police not finding the crowbar at the warehouse. After all, he was living at Beej's house when he was arrested. And it was possible that the coins the police had found had fallen out in his backpack and Nick hadn't noticed.

"Nick, if there's anything you haven't told anybody about what happened and why it happened," I said, choosing my words carefully, "you should tell it now.

The police want to get to the truth. I know they do. You could talk to your lawyer. Or to my dad." Or to me, I thought, even though I seemed to be the last person he wanted to confide in. "He likes you. If there's anything he can do to help, I know he'll do it."

"What are you talking about, Robyn?" he said. Then realization—and disappointment—appeared in his eyes. "You really think I did it, don't you?" He shook his head.

"I know how you feel about Mr. Schuster, Nick. I know you wouldn't do anything to hurt him. But it looks bad." I hesitated, but I had to know. "The police said you had a thousand dollars on you when you were arrested and that you refused to say where it came from."

He seemed surprised that I knew. "That was my money."

"Where did you get it?"

"That's none of your business."

"Right."

He slumped back in the recliner. His eyes went to the ring on my finger. "You used to trust me. When did you stop? When you met that guy?"

"I want to help you, Nick. But I can't do it alone. You have to help yourself."

"That's exactly what I'm going to do, Robyn—help myself. I don't need you."

He switched on the TV and stared stubbornly at it. I couldn't get another word out of him.

. . .

Beej was huddled in the doorway to my father's building when I got home.

"Where have you been?" she said. "Didn't school get out hours ago?"

"I have a life," I said curtly. I couldn't help it. Seeing her gave me pangs of jealousy. "What do you want?"

"I thought maybe you'd been trying to reach me— you know, to let me know if you'd talked to Nick. But our phone got trashed along with everything else. I checked our messages from another phone, but there was nothing from you. So then I thought maybe when our phone got messed up, it affected our voice mail."

"What do you mean, your phone got trashed? What happened?"

"Someone broke into our place. They tossed all the drawers and closets, ripped open all the mattresses, and smashed up the phone. But it's not like we have anything worth stealing. We think maybe it was some crack addict. So did you see Nick?"

I nodded.

"And?"

"And why didn't you tell me he had a thousand dollars in cash when he was arrested?"

"What does that have to do with anything?"

"Beej, he was living in an abandoned building, but he had all that cash? That didn't seem strange to you?"

"No. Why would it?"

"When was the last time Nick had that much money on him?"

95

"He told me a girl gave it to him."

"A girl?"

"Yeah. While he was hitching home, he found some girl's purse. When he returned it, she gave him a reward."

"A thousand dollars?"

"That's what Nick told me."

"Some girl gave him a thousand dollars. In cash." I said.

She nodded.

"Come on. You actually believe that?"

"Why wouldn't I?" she said, glowering at me. "He said that when he returned that purse, he was just doing what anyone would have done and he didn't feel right about taking a reward. He said he was gonna give it back."

"Oh. So this girl lives around here? What's her name?"

"Sarah something. I don't know. Nick didn't tell me her last name. He said she was on her way to Europe."

No wonder he didn't want to tell the police that story. I was skeptical, and I *wanted* to believe him.

"So exactly how was he planning to return the money to this mystery girl?" I said.

"He gave her his aunt's phone number. He said the girl was going to leave a message for him there when she got back to town." She glared at me. "You think he's lying, don't you?"

"About the money? You have to admit, it sounds pretty far-fetched."

She shook her head in disgust. "I thought you were his friend."

· · ·

"You're a hard person to get hold of," Ben said when I called him again from my father's place.

"I'm sorry. I forgot to recharge my phone."

"I feel like I haven't seen you in ages."

"It's only been a couple of days. Morgan and I have been slaving over our project." Well, Morgan had been slaving. I was starting to feel guilty about how little I had done.

"Oh, well. A couple more days and it'll be March break. I can't wait. I miss you."

"Miss you too," I said. I thought when I said it that I meant it, but for some reason, the words didn't ring true in my ears.

· · ·

"You're ditching class?" Morgan said the next morning when I told her why I couldn't meet for lunch.

"Technically, no," I said. "I have a free period after lunch, and I'll be back in time for my next class." I filled her in on what I had overheard on Mr. Schuster's phone. "I have to find out what's going on, Morgan."

It had eaten at me all night. Nick had seemed so disappointed at the thought that I didn't believe him. He'd said that he didn't want my help, that he was going to take care of things himself. What if he did something foolish? What if he ended up in more trouble?

Morgan looked doubtful. "It's a big mall, Robyn."

"I know exactly where he's going to be."

She checked her watch. "Well, we'd better get going if we're going to make it on time."

"*We?* You're going to ditch class?"

"I just remembered that I have a dentist appointment. And my dentist's office is at the mall."

"You need a note for that."

"No problem," she said, grinning. "I'm sure I can come up with one."

We made it to the mall with ten minutes to spare. The Gap was on the second floor. We were hurrying toward the escalator when Morgan pointed up: "There he is!"

I scanned the knots of shoppers on the second floor. Nick was walking quickly toward the Gap, which was to the left of the escalator. Elliot was nowhere in sight, but a moment later, I saw Isobel and her grandfather. They were near the top of the escalator. Mr. Schuster was clutching his walker. Isobel was holding his arm to support him. At first I was afraid that Isobel was going to try to take Schuster down the escalator, which wouldn't be safe. Then I saw her point to something farther on. The glass-walled elevator just past the escalators? She seemed to be steering him in that direction.

Just as Isobel and Mr. Schuster were making their way past the top of the escalator, Nick ran up behind them. I couldn't tell if they had seen him or not—there were a lot of people pressing to get on the escalator, and I lost them for a moment. When I caught sight of Isobel again, she seemed to be struggling to maneuver her grandfather away from the top of the escalator. A look on her face told me that something was wrong. Mr. Schuster was having trouble with his walker.

Nick had moved directly behind the two of them. I thought he was going to say something to Mr. Schuster, but instead he turned his head. While I watched, he thrust his hands out in front of him. Then—oh my God!—Mr. Schuster lurched forward and down the escalator. Isobel screamed and scrambled to grab him, but she wasn't fast enough. Mr. Schuster slammed into the man in front of him. The other man jerking aside, turning to see what had happened. The look of annoyance on the man's face quickly turned to alarm. The man tried to get hold of Mr. Schuster, but with no one in front of him anymore to break his fall, Mr. Schuster continued to pitch forward. I watched in horror as he fell all the way down the escalator. His walker clattered down in front of him.

Some quick-thinking person at the bottom hit the emergency Stop button. The escalator ground to a halt, forcing the people behind Mr. Schuster to clutch the handrail to keep themselves from careening forward. More people crowded around the spot where Schuster lay crumpled on the ground.

"Did you see that?" Morgan said, her eyes wide with astonishment. "Did you see what I saw?"

I nodded grimly. I didn't want to believe it, but I had seen it.

"Nick pushed that man," Morgan said. "He pushed him right down the escalator."

"That man is Mr. Schuster," I said.

"What?" Morgan looked stunned. "Are you sure? Why would Nick push Mr. Schuster down the escalator?"

How could I possibly answer that question? I could barely believe it had happened.

People in the crowd were talking and pointing at Nick, who stood frozen at the top of the stalled escalator. He didn't resist when a man grabbed him and held him. A security guard appeared at the bottom of the escalator. He knelt down to check on Mr. Schuster and then spoke into a walkie-talkie.

The man who had grabbed Nick hauled him down the escalator and dragged him over to the security guard. I saw Nick shake his head. Isobel stared up at him, disbelief in her eyes. The security guard stood up and took Nick by the arm. Then Elliot appeared. He bounded down the escalator and knelt down beside his father. He said something to Isobel, who was crying. She shook her head. I have no idea what she said, but Elliot sprang to his feet and flew at Nick. A second security guard appeared. The two guards pulled Elliot off Nick. Then one of them twisted Nick's arms behind his back and handcuffed him.

"Can mall cops make arrests?" Morgan said.

"In the mall they can," I said, still in a daze. I watched the first guard speak into his walkie-talkie again. Elliot crouched down beside Mr. Schuster. He put his arm around Isobel. Their backs were to us. A moment later, yet another security guard arrived. Two of the guards started talking to people. They were probably trying to piece together who had seen what. The third one kept a firm grip on Nick.

One of the guards came over to where Morgan and I were standing.

"Excuse me, ladies," he said. Morgan winced at the word ladies. "Did you see what happened on the escalator?"

Morgan glanced at me. Her face twisted with indecision. I decided to put her out of her agony.

"Yes, we did," I said.

"Then I'm going to ask you to stay here. The police are on their way, and they're going to want to talk to everyone who witnessed the incident."

I nodded and glanced over to where Nick was standing. He was staring at me. He did not look happy to see me.

The police arrived five minutes later. So did the paramedics. The police spoke to Elliot while the paramedics attended to Mr. Schuster. When they lifted Mr. Schuster onto a gurney and started to wheel him away, Elliot and Isobel went with them. Police officers began to interview the people the security guards had asked to stay.

"It looked to me like Nick pushed the old man," Morgan said when a uniformed officer finally got to us. Her cheeks flushed as soon as she realized what she had said.

"You know the accused?" the officer said.

"Sort of," Morgan said. "I've seen him around."

The police officer looked at me. "What about you? Did you see what happened?"

I nodded. "He—Nick—was on the escalator behind Mr. Schuster—"

The police officer's eyes narrowed. "You know the victim?"

"I walk his dog for him," I said.

He nodded, but I bet he was thinking it was quite a coincidence that Morgan and I had witnessed the incident. "Go on," he said.

"Well . . ." I hesitated. My father once told me that police officers are naturally suspicious. A good officer questions everything. This one was looking at me as if I were an unreliable witness, as if it had crossed his mind that I might be biased in some way. "It did look like Nick pushed Mr. Schuster. But I could be wrong."

"Why do you say that?"

I wanted to say, "Because Nick likes Mr. Schuster and would never hurt him." But I couldn't tell the police officer that without admitting how well I knew Nick. What if Elliot found out? Instead, I said, "It all happened so fast."

"Can you describe exactly what you saw?" he said.

I said that Nick had been at the top of the escalator behind Mr. Schuster and Isobel; that I had seen him raise both hands in front of him; that it looked like he had made contact with Mr. Schuster; and that right after that, Mr. Schuster had fallen.

"So you're saying that the accused pushed the victim?" the police officer said.

"It sort of looked like it," I said.

"Sort of? You either saw him push that man or you didn't."

"I guess I saw him," I admitted.

After double-checking our names, addresses, and phone numbers, he said we could go.

"I know I saw it," Morgan said as we headed for the mall exit. "But I still don't believe it."

That was the thing—neither did I.

CHAPTER **TEN**

We got back to school nearly an hour after lunch period had ended. Mr. Dormer, one of the vice principals, stopped me and Morgan and asked us to account for our absence. Morgan didn't have to use her dentist appointment excuse. Instead, she told the truth: we had gone to the mall, had witnessed an assault, and were detained because the police wanted us to make a statement. She even gave him the badge number of the police officer we had been talking to.

I had history and French that afternoon. I must even have listened because I scribbled a couple of pages of notes. But I don't remember my teachers saying what I wrote down. My mind kept playing back what I had seen at the mall. Had I been wrong about Nick going to meet Elliot? Had he really gone there to see Mr. Schuster? But why would he risk detention by breaking bail? More importantly, why would he push Mr. Schuster down the escalator? Nick had been in fights before. I knew that. But he would never attack a helpless old man. He just wouldn't. I felt sure of that—even though I had witnessed the whole incident. There had to be some other explanation.

As soon as school was over, I hurried to Mr. Schuster's house. No one answered when I rang the bell. Poor Orion. He would have to stay shut up in the basement this afternoon. I was turning to go when Connor slouched up the front walk, shivering in a light canvas jacket, his gloveless hands jammed into the pockets.

"My parents are at the hospital with my grandpa," he said. "That guy Nick—he pushed Grandpa down an escalator."

"Is your grandfather okay?" I said.

"I don't know," he said. "My parents were waiting to talk to the doctor. My dad sent me back to let you in so you could walk the dog." His hands shook as he unlocked the front door.

"You must be cold," I said, trying to be pleasant.

"My mom got one of the neighbors to drive us to the hospital," he said. "I wasn't expecting to have to come home on the bus." He pushed the door open and I followed him inside. Orion's barking filled the house. "I hope Grandpa doesn't have to stay there for long," he said. "Before he came home last time, that dog never shut up. He barked all night. I couldn't sleep."

"I'm sure Orion will be better after he's had a walk," I said. I headed for the basement door. Connor immediately retreated to the living room, closing the French doors behind him. When I came back up with Orion, Connor was at the farthest end of the couch, watching the dog's every move. I felt sorry for him, but I felt sorrier for Orion. After Nick and Mr. Schuster had trained Orion at the animal shelter last summer, he had gotten used to a new, happy life with Mr. Schuster. For him to be locked in a dark basement all day must have been as bad as being in prison.

I took Orion for a long walk and ran willingly after him as he chased squirrel after squirrel. I noted with satisfaction that he walked much slower beside me on the way home than he had on the way to the park. He would sleep well.

I'd been hoping that the Schusters would be home when I got back to the house so that I could find out how Mr. Schuster was doing. But there was just Connor, still parked in front of the TV, watching cartoons. He watched as I led a reluctant Orion back down to the basement. Before I left, I asked him which hospital Mr. Schuster was in.

. . .

My father wasn't home when I got there, but he called shortly after I arrived to tell me he wouldn't be home for supper.

"There's plenty of food in the fridge," he said. "Or you can go downstairs and get Fred to feed you. I should be back around nine or ten."

He didn't tell me why he was going to be late, and I didn't ask. Whenever my father doesn't volunteer that information, it usually means he's on a job. When he's on a job, it's always confidential.

Morgan called a few minutes later.

"So?" she said. "Did you find out anything?"

"Like what?" I said.

"Like what Nick was doing at the mall in the first place? Like why he pushed Mr. Schuster?"

"How am I supposed to find that out? They arrested Nick. If he isn't still in detention, for sure his aunt has him under lock and key." The day's events flashed before my eyes again. "I still can't believe . . ."

"But we saw it, Robyn. We both did."

We had both seen Nick behind Mr. Schuster. We had both seen him thrust his hands out. We had both seen Mr. Schuster fall. But it didn't make any sense—not to me, anyway.

Then something hit me—I hadn't heard the phone at Mr. Schuster's house ring that afternoon.

. . .

I should have worked on my project. As it was, it would be a miracle if it got finished before spring break. But I couldn't concentrate. When my dad got home, he found me staring up at the moon through the skylight above the dining table. He sank down onto a chair opposite me. He looked exhausted.

"Tough day?" I said.

"And then some. How about you?"

"My day kind of sucked too," I said. I told him what had happened at the mall.

"You keep saying it *looked* like Nick pushed Schuster," he said when I had finished.

I had said the same thing to the cop who had interviewed Morgan and me.

"Are you hesitating because you're not sure about what you saw or because you don't want to believe it?"

"I don't know," I admitted. "Morgan is sure she saw Nick push him. She doesn't understand why he did it, but she's positive that's what happened."

"But you're not?"

He peered at me, waiting for an answer.

"I guess not," I said. "I wish I could see it again. I wish I could see it in slow motion. What do you think is going to happen, Dad? Will they keep him locked up, or will they let him go back to his aunt's place?"

"He broke bail, Robbie. And he's facing another charge. It will take some convincing to get him released."

"Is there any way I can see him?"

"Even if it were possible, I don't think it would be a very good idea."

"Why not?"

"The charges against him are serious. You were a witness to what happened today. You gave a statement to the police. That means you're involved. If this ends up in court, you could be called as a witness."

"I'm worried about him, Dad."

My father sighed as he got to his feet. "It's late, and it's been a long day. I need to get some sleep." He started for his room, then paused and turned back to me. "What exactly were you doing at the mall, Robbie?"

I hadn't told the police that I'd overheard Nick make plans to meet someone there because I didn't want to be the one who made it worse for him. I didn't tell my dad for the same reason.

"Morgan had a dentist appointment," I said. "I went with her."

"It was just a coincidence that you happened to witness what you did?"

I nodded. I don't know whether my dad believed me or not, but he didn't ask any more questions.

I stayed up for longer than I should have. I thought about the phone that hadn't rung. That had to mean that someone in Mr. Schuster's house had called Nick and not the other way around. Had it been Elliot? If that were true, why had Nick run to catch up with Mr. Schuster and Isobel?

I knocked on the door to my father's bedroom. He groaned but sat up and turned on the light.

"Having trouble sleeping?" he said, his eyes bleary, his hair sticking out all over his head.

"I need a favor."

He listened in silence to my request. To my surprise, he didn't argue with me. He didn't quiz me. In fact, he didn't give me any grief at all. Instead, he said, "I'll see what I can do."

. . .

School let out at noon the next day. It was the beginning of break. I decided to use the extra time that afternoon to go to the hospital and see Mr. Schuster. Morgan came with me.

"Robyn!" someone called just as we stepped off the elevator. "Robyn!"

It was Isobel. She was in a small waiting room across from the elevator. So were some of Mr. Schuster's neighbors—Esther and Edith and another woman I recognized from my dog-walking expeditions. Isobel's parents stood halfway down the hall talking to a man in a white lab coat. Isobel came out of the waiting room to greet me.

"How's your grandfather?" I asked.

"My dad said nothing is broken, so I guess that's good," she said. "But he hurt his wrists and his back and one of his knees got banged up. It's really swollen. The doctor says that in his condition, it could take a long time for him to recover. Depending on how much damage was done to his knee and his back, he might not be able to walk again for a long time." Tears welled up in her eyes. "After all that progress he made . . ."

"It looks like he's had a lot of visitors," I said gently. "I bet he appreciates that."

Isobel nodded. "All of those women in there are either neighbors or they know him from church. My dad says he had no idea Grandpa was such a ladies' man."

"Will he be able to go home soon?"

Isobel's face clouded again.

"That's what my parents are talking to Grandpa's doctor about. The doctor is worried. He thinks Grandpa should consider going to a home, where he can be looked after. But Grandpa doesn't want that. He got all upset when my dad mentioned it. My parents got into a big argument about it. My dad keeps saying that Grandpa isn't well enough to make decisions for himself, but he doesn't want to force him into a nursing home. My mom thinks my dad should take charge and that if the doctor thinks Grandpa needs to be in a nursing home, then that's what he should do."

I glanced at Elliot, who was shaking the doctor's hand.

"Isobel," I said, "what were you—"

I stopped when I spotted Elliot and Claudia coming toward us.

"Robyn," Elliot said. "I understand you were at the mall yesterday. One of the police officers I spoke to said that he took a statement from the girl who walks my dad's dog."

Isobel stared at me.

"You were there?" she said.

"I was doing some errands with my friend." I nodded at Morgan.

"It's quite a coincidence that you witnessed the whole thing," Elliot said. "The police told me they took a lot of statements. If they don't lock up that boy, then there's something seriously wrong with our justice system."

Morgan glanced at me.

"Is your father well enough to have visitors?" I asked.

"I'm sure he'd love to see you," Isobel said before Elliot could answer. "Come on. I'll take you."

Morgan shrugged, slipped into the waiting room, and started sorting through a stack of dog-eared magazines. Mr. Schuster opened his eyes as soon as he heard us enter the room. He looked right at me, then touched the bridge of his nose and traced a line diagonally across his cheek to the bottom of his ear.

"He wants to know how Nick is," Isobel said.

"I haven't seen him," I said. I turned to Isobel. "Did you take your grandfather to the mall to see Nick?"

Isobel's cheeks turned pink. She bit her lower lip and glanced at her grandfather. He nodded.

"Did Nick ask you to meet him there?"

"No," she said. "I called him."

I had been right. The phone hadn't rung because Nick wasn't the one who made the call.

"Grandpa asked me to. At first he wanted me to see how Nick was doing. Then he wanted me to arrange for him to see him. But every time I called, a man answered and told me that Nick couldn't come to the phone."

That explained why Glen had told me to stop calling the one time I'd tried to get Nick on the phone. He must have mistaken me for Isobel. But Isobel had finally got through.

"Do you know why your grandfather wanted to see Nick?"

Isobel glanced at her grandfather again. Again, he nodded.

"He wanted me to ask Nick if he stole those coins. He wanted to look at Nick when he answered. He knew he'd be able to tell if Nick was telling the truth."

Mr. Schuster nodded.

"And?" I said.

Mr. Schuster shook his head slowly.

"We didn't have a chance to talk to Nick before Grandpa . . . before he fell," Isobel said.

I looked into Mr. Schuster's watery eyes.

"Do you think Nick pushed you?" I said.

He neither nodded nor shook his head. Either he didn't know or he didn't want to say. I don't think he wanted to believe that Nick would hurt him.

"What about you, Isobel?" I said. "What do you think?"

She looked uncertain. "I don't know."

.   .   .

"Now what?" Morgan said when I went back to the waiting room.

Good question. I was both relieved and puzzled by what Isobel had told me. Nick hadn't gone to the mall to meet Elliot. And it seemed less likely that he had gone to harm Mr. Schuster. Instead, he had gone because Mr. Schuster, through Isobel, had asked him to. But I was still haunted by what I had seen at the mall and I wondered, not for the first time that day, whether my father had had a chance to do what I had asked. But even if he had, it wouldn't explain what had happened to Mr. Schuster's coin collection. Maybe I had been wrong about what had brought Nick to the mall, but that didn't mean I had been wrong about everything. I thought about what Esther and Edith had said about Elliot asking his parents for money and about what I had overheard Claudia say about credit cards. I also thought about Elliot's insistence that his father wasn't well enough to make his own decisions. Add to all of that his sudden interest in his father's coin collection—and his knowledge of Nick's past . . .

Another picture started to emerge. What if Elliot was scheming to get control of his father's affairs, including his financial affairs? What if he'd come up with a way to get his hands on both the coin collection and the insurance money—by making Nick look like a thief? It would explain a lot of what had happened. But how could I prove it?

"Robyn?" Morgan said, elbowing me.

"Huh?"

"What are you going to do now?"

"I need to talk to Elliot. I'll be right back."

I got up and went back out into the hall. Elliot and Claudia were standing outside Mr. Schuster's room, deep in conversation.

"Oh, yes, the dog," Elliot said when I asked him. "We'll be here for a while, but Connor is at the house. He'll let you in."

Perfect, I thought. I waved Morgan out of the waiting room and told her I was going to go walk Orion.

"So I guess I'll catch up with you later, then," she said.

"Uh-uh. You're coming with me. I need you to help create a diversion."

"Diversion?"

While we waited for the bus, I explained to her what I had been thinking. Morgan was intrigued.

"But what about what happened at the mall?" she said.

"I'm working on that." Or, rather, I hoped my father was.

As the bus pulled up in front of us, my phone rang. It was Ben.

"You want to do something tonight?" he said.

"Uh, okay," I said. I hadn't given Ben much thought lately. I had been too preoccupied with Nick. He must have picked up on my mood because he said, "Is everything okay, Robyn?"

"Sure. Everything's fine."

We made plans to see a movie. Morgan looked quizzically at me when I dropped my phone back into my pocket, but she didn't ask.

After a short ride on the bus, we got off and walked to Mr. Schuster's house. I was about to ring the bell when Morgan put out a hand to stop me.

"Just a sec," she said. She pulled a compact mirror out of her bag, checked her reflection, then freshened her mascara. "Okay. Ready."

As Elliot had promised, Connor let us in. He quietly acknowledged me but couldn't take his eyes off Morgan. She's what most people would call beautiful. She knows it, and she's not above using it to her advantage—or mine, if I ask. She flashed Connor a great big smile and thrust out a hand. He puffed up a little when she asked him what his sport was.

"How do you know I'm into sports?" he said, cheeks flushing.

"Are you kidding?" Morgan said. "The shape you're in, either you're into sports or you work out on the reg."

"I'm gonna go and get Orion," I said—not that anyone was listening.

"Football," Connor said. "And I play hockey."

I headed for the basement. Orion jumped up at the barrier when he heard me coming.

"Hey, boy," I said, holding out a dog biscuit. He devoured it and barked. He seemed more worked up than usual. He probably missed his visits with Mr. Schuster. I removed his leash from the hook and pushed the barrier aside. Orion wriggled through the opening before I could attach the leash and bolted up the stairs. I ran after him, but I wasn't fast enough.

"Hey!" Connor shouted in alarm.

By the time I reached the top of the stairs, Connor was plastered against the wall, his eyes wide with terror. Orion was in front of him, barking furiously. Morgan was off to one side, staring steadfastly at the floor. She didn't know Orion, but she did know better than to stare a strange dog in the eyes. The dog might take that as a challenge.

"Orion," I said. "Sit."

Instead, Orion turned and streaked up the stairs. This was not going according to plan.

"Catch him!" Connor screamed at me. "Put him back in the basement."

I glanced at Morgan. She took Connor by the hand.

"It's okay," she said calmly. "Robyn knows what she's doing." She shot me a glance that told me that she hoped so. She led Connor toward the living room, and he darted inside gratefully. Morgan mouthed "Good luck" at me from behind the room's French doors. I had a feeling I was going to need it. Morgan was doing her part, but Orion was not cooperating. He was really wound up.

The barking stopped just as I got to the top of the stairs. Orion wasn't in the hallway, which meant that he was in one of the rooms. I pictured him lurking in a doorway, ready to pounce.

Get a grip, I told myself. Orion might not be perfect, but he wasn't vicious, either, no matter what Connor thought. Second, dogs can sense fear. I told myself to think of something pleasant, something that would calm me. An image flashed into my mind: Nick and me cuddling together on my father's couch.

It was like a blow to the heart.

All of a sudden, I realized that I wasn't mad at Nick anymore. I missed him. I wanted to be with him. If only he wasn't in so much trouble . . .

I drew myself straight and reminded myself that I was upstairs for a reason. I stood silently in the hall and listened for Orion. A whimpering sound was coming from Mr. Schuster's bedroom. I peeked inside. Orion was lying on Mr. Schuster's bed. His head was flopped on a pillow.

I approached him cautiously and sat down on the bed beside him. He looked at me with sad eyes. I held my hand out so that he could sniff it, then patted his head. He whimpered again.

"I know exactly how you feel," I said. I patted him some more and then snapped the leash onto his collar. "Come on. We've got work to do, and then I'll take you for a nice, long walk."

His ears pricked up when he heard the word *walk*. He jumped off the bed and padded down the hall with me. Connor and Morgan were still locked away in the living room. Connor's eyes got big when he caught sight of Orion coming down the stairs. Then Morgan reached out and touched his arm, and Connor seemed to forget that there was anyone else in the house.

When we got to the bottom of the stairs, I slipped a few Kanine Kookies out of my pocket. After a quick glance to make sure Connor wasn't looking, I threw them into Mr. Schuster's den and let go of Orion's leash. The big dog bolted through the den door to hunt for the biscuits.

"Oh, no!" I cried. Connor's eyes widened again at the sound of my voice. "Don't worry. I'll get him," I said. I darted into the den after Orion.

Orion had finished one of the three biscuits I had tossed into the room and was sniffing around for another one. I left him to it and crossed to the desk. Elliot was running his business from here, he'd told me. Just like the last time I'd been in Mr. Schuster's den, the desk was piled with file folders and business papers. I was distracted for a few moments by a copy of the police report on Nick's arrest that was lying on top of the pile. I scanned it quickly, absorbing a few details that were new to me. It didn't sound good. Nick would need a very good lawyer if these charges went to court. I set the report aside and shuffled through the rest of the papers as quickly as I could, not at all sure what I was looking for—not until I found it.

It was a file folder with several letters inside. Elliot owed the bank a lot of money. And he'd been turned down for a loan by a number of other banks. His business was in trouble. That would certainly give him a motive for cashing in on his father's coin collection.

"No, I don't think we need to call animal control," I heard Morgan say loudly. "I'm sure Robyn has everything under control. *Don't you, Robyn?*"

Orion was happily crunching on the last of the biscuits I had tossed into the den. I hastily put the file folder back where I had found it, grabbed the end of Orion's leash, and wrapped it around my wrist.

"Time for a walk," I said, my voice as loud as Morgan's had been. I led him out of the den.

Connor was still safely behind the French doors with Morgan when Orion and I stepped out into the front hall.

"See?" Morgan said, standing up. She smiled sweetly. Connor looked as if he were going to melt. He opened his mouth to say something but clamped it shut again when Morgan opened the French doors to let herself out. Connor watched longingly as she pulled on her coat and boots. But his fear of dogs must have got the better of him, because he stayed put and waved reluctantly as we headed for the door and let ourselves out.

"So?" Morgan said eagerly as soon as we were out on the porch. "Did you find anything that might help Nick? Were you—"

The words died in her throat as the front door swung open. Connor was standing there with a love-struck look on his face that vanished as he absorbed what he had just heard. Or, I hoped, maybe he hadn't heard anything at all.

"Come on, Morgan," I said quickly. "Let's go." I turned to leave—and found myself face-to-face with the man who had come looking for Mrs. Schuster a few days back. He gave me an odd look, as if he thought he knew me but couldn't place me.

"Is Claudia Schuster here?" he said. As soon as he spoke, Orion started to bark. The man stepped back. His expression cleared. "You're the brave young lady who walks the dog," he said, smiling at me.

"Mrs. Schuster isn't home," I said. "But this is her son. He can probably let you know when she's going to be back."

I tugged on Orion's leash, and we marched down the front walk without once looking back.

"Slow down," Morgan said when we finally reached the street.

I shook my head. "I hope Connor didn't hear what you said, Morgan. If Elliot finds out I know Nick, he won't let me in the house again. And I'm already worried about what they're going to do to Orion, especially if they put Mr. Schuster in a nursing home."

"I'm sure he didn't hear anything," Morgan said. "If he had, he would have said something."

"Maybe," I said. But maybe not.

"You weren't kidding about him. What a wuss. I think he'd even be afraid of Missy." Missy was Morgan's black Lab, the sweetest dog on the planet.

"To be fair, he was mauled by a Rottweiler," I said. "But between him and his mother . . ."

My phone rang. It was my dad. "How soon can you get to the mall?" he said.

CHAPTER **ELEVEN**

"Is he taking you shopping?" Morgan said when I told her I had to meet my father.

I filled her in. She looked dubiously at Orion.

"What about him?" she said.

"I don't suppose you could walk him and then take him home?"

She looked at the big dog and shook her head. "You know I'd do anything for you, Robyn, but—"

I didn't blame her. "It's okay. I'll take him with me for now."

.   .   .

My dad was waiting at the bottom of the escalator where Mr. Schuster had fallen. He looked from Orion to me.

"Will he behave?" he asked.

"Yes," I said. At least, I hoped so.

"Okay, follow me." He led the way across the main floor and down a narrow corridor to a door marked: Security. Authorized Personnel Only. He rapped on the door. A uniformed guard opened it.

My father introduced himself. "Mr. Logan is expecting me," he said.

The security guard showed us into a room filled with wall-mounted TV monitors. A middle-aged man who had been watching the monitors stood up to greet us.

"Mac," he said, pumping my father's hand. "Long time no see."

"How's the private sector treating you, Walt?" my father said.

"Can't complain. I hear you're doing well."

"Guess I can't complain, either." My father grinned and introduced me. Then he said, "About that footage I asked you about . . ."

"I'm surprised no one else has asked me about it yet," Walt said.

"The injuries weren't life-threatening," my father said. "I'm sure they'll get around to it."

Walt took a DVD from his desk and popped it into a player on the other side of the room. We gathered around a TV next to it. I told Orion to sit. He obeyed immediately. I could have kissed him. Then I held my breath as Walt pressed Play.

"Okay," Walt said. "This is your guy, right?" He pointed to Nick standing at the top of the escalator.

"That's him," my father said.

When I had witnessed what had happened, I'd been at the bottom of the escalator, looking up from one side. The camera angle was completely different. It caught the action head on, and this time I saw things that I hadn't seen the first time. Mr. Schuster shuffled into the frame, leaning heavily on his walker. Isobel was holding his arm. She was frowning. People were coming at them from all directions, heading for the escalator. She and Mr. Schuster got separated, and Schuster seemed to be having trouble navigating his way through all the people. He got dangerously close to the top of the escalator. Then Nick came up behind Mr. Schuster and Isobel. Isobel turned, still frowning, and said something to him. She pointed to her left and started to help Mr. Schuster away from the top of the escalator. It looked like Nick was trying to give her a hand.

"He's being awfully helpful to someone he intends to push, isn't he?" Walt said.

My father didn't answer. His eyes were fixed on the screen. So were mine.

Suddenly the expression on Nick's face changed. He cocked his head and frowned, as if he had heard something. Then it happened. Nick thrust out his hands. They rammed into Mr. Schuster's back. Mr. Schuster lurched forward and toppled down the escalator.

"Let me see that again," my dad said.

Walt stopped and rewound. This time he slowed the footage down. We all leaned forward to get a better look. We must have watched it half a dozen times, Walt playing the scene frame by frame when my father asked him to, before I was sure about what I was seeing. Yes, Nick had pushed Mr. Schuster. But I could see why. A man in a wide-brimmed hat darted in front of someone else to get directly behind Nick. Nick turned his head toward the man. Then, for no reason that I could see, the man rammed Nick with one shoulder, throwing him off balance and propelling him violently forward. Both of Nick's hands flew out in front of him—and sent Mr. Schuster reeling.

Then Mr. Schuster fell into a man who moved aside, realized what was happening, and tried too late to help. The other people on the escalator turned and watched, too surprised to do anything. Once Schuster reached the bottom of the escalator, a man hit the emergency Stop button. Isobel scrambled to the bottom to see if Schuster was all right. Nick stood where he was, seemingly stunned. When he started down the escalator, a man grabbed him and held him. The rest of the people walked to the bottom of the escalator and stood around, some of them looking at Mr. Schuster, a few of them pointing at Nick.

"Nick didn't push Mr. Schuster," I said. "Someone pushed Nick. It almost looked like he did it on purpose."

I glanced at my father. He was staring intently at the TV screen.

"Stop," he said. "Rewind a little and play it again."

Walt did as he was asked.

"Pause it," my father said. "There. Look at that."

We all peered at the screen. Walt nodded.

"What exactly are we looking at?" I said.

My father pointed to the man in the wide-brimmed hat. His head was bowed, making it impossible to see his face underneath his overcoat.

"That's the man who bumped into Nick," I said.

"See what he's doing?" my father said.

I looked at the screen again

"He isn't doing anything," I said. "He's just walking away."

"Exactly," my father said. "Everyone on the escalator stopped to see how Mr. Schuster was. That man just kept going. He didn't even look at Schuster. If he'd tripped or fell against Nick, if the whole thing was an accident, you'd expect him to stop. You'd at least expect him to look at what he'd done, even if he didn't want to take responsibility."

"Or if someone else was being blamed," Walt said grimly.

"So you don't think it was an accident," I said. "You think that man pushed Nick on purpose."

My dad nodded.

"But why?" I said. "I don't get it."

"Neither do I," my father said. "But it's obvious from this tape that Nick fell against Schuster. He didn't push him. That part was an accident. The man who pushed Nick, though—that's another story." He looked at Walt. "Will you call the police?" he said. "Tell them about the footage. Make sure they get a copy."

"Sure thing," Walt said.

"And if it's not too much trouble, could you make a copy for me?"

Walt smiled and hit the Eject button. When the DVD popped out, he dropped it into a plastic case and handed it to my dad.

"Did that right after I called you," he said.

"What are you going to do now?" I asked my dad after we left the security office.

"I'm going to take this to Nick's lawyer. It will definitely help him."

"You think the police will drop the charge against him?"

"I would think you can count on it."

"Will they release him?"

My dad was less certain about that. "Maybe he didn't push Mr. Schuster on purpose," he said. "But he did break the terms of his bail." He sighed. "I have to get going, Robbie. I'll see you later, okay?"

"I'm going out with Ben tonight."

"In that case, I'll see you when you get home."

After my father left, I took Orion for a long walk. After that, there was no avoiding it. He had to go back to Mr. Schuster's.

. . .

Mr. Schuster's front door swung open before I had a chance to knock. Elliot and Claudia stared out at me.

"I'm surprised you had the nerve to come back here," Elliot said.

"I took Orion for his walk, just like I told you," I said. When he heard the word *walk*, Orion barked. Claudia edged behind her husband.

"You have to do something about that animal, Elliot," she said.

"He's a good dog," I said. "But he's also a big dog. He needs plenty of exercise. He's not used to being cooped up in the basement all the time."

"Thank you, but I don't think we need your advice," Elliot said stiffly. He handed me an envelope. "Your services are no longer needed. This is what I owe you. You deceived me, Robyn. You led me to believe that you're a friend of my father's—"

"I am."

"You conveniently forgot to mention that you're also a friend of that young thief. You told Connor that you didn't know Nick, but Connor told me what he heard your friend say this afternoon."

I opened my mouth to say something, but Elliot cut me off. A telephone rang.

"Don't bother to deny it," he said. "You also told Connor that someone at the animal shelter told you that my father was sick. Well, I called the shelter. They didn't even know he was ill. He hasn't been there in months. Neither have you. I also asked them about your background. They said you and Nick are friends. But you're more than friends, aren't you?" My cheeks turned red.

Isobel came down the stairs. She must have over-heard her father because she looked embarrassed. She mouthed a word: *Sorry*.

"Mom," she said. "Telephone for you."

Claudia looked relieved to have an excuse to duck into the den. She closed the door behind her. I turned back to Elliot.

"I know Nick," I admitted. "But I didn't lie about being a friend of your father's. I am. When I heard he was sick—"

"Nick told you, didn't he?" Elliot said. "Did he also tell you to come here? Are you looking for something else to steal?"

"No. I—"

He held the door open for me.

"Good night," he said firmly.

I handed him Orion's leash. Orion growled. Elliot stiffened. Orion growled again and jumped up on Elliot. As Elliot dropped the leash, I scooped it up.

"Do you want me to put him in the basement for you?" I said.

Elliot hesitated a moment before stepping aside to let me enter. I kept a firm grip on Orion's leash while I pulled off my boots.

Elliot crossed his arms and watched me lead Orion into the basement. When I emerged a couple of minutes later, he looked like he hadn't moved a muscle.

"If you call the animal shelter, they should be able to refer you to a dog-walking service," I said.

Elliot didn't acknowledge the suggestion. While I was putting my boots back on, Claudia came out of the den. She still looked nervous, even though the dog was safely in the basement.

"Who was that?" Elliot asked her.

"Someone from one of the nursing homes I called earlier," Claudia said. Her eyes darted to me for a moment. "They're going to send us some information."

Elliot opened the door for me. I hated to leave Orion there alone. I hoped he would be okay.

It was dark by the time I left the Schuster house. I glanced at my watch as I hurried up the street. *I should call Ben*, I thought, *and tell him I might be a little late.* I was out of breath by the time I reached the bus stop in front of a boarded-up corner store two blocks from Mr. Schuster's house. It was freezing out and the wind was harsh. There were houses nearby, but there were hardly any lights on in any of them.

Somewhere behind me, I heard a car door slam, but I didn't think anything of it. I started to slip my backpack off my shoulder so that I could get my phone out. Started but never finished, because someone grabbed me from behind and clapped a hand over my mouth. The next thing I knew, I was being dragged down the alley that ran alongside the abandoned store.

CHAPTER **TWELVE**

I tried to dig my heels in, but the arms around me were too strong, and the street grew more and more distant. So I fought back. At least, I tried to.

I lashed out with both hands, trying to strike backward at my attacker. He wrapped a powerful arm around me, pinning both my arms to my sides.

I kicked at him and landed a blow on one of his shins. He muttered a curse. The arm that had been pinning me suddenly released me. Adrenaline surged through me. Maybe I could break free. Maybe I could run. Then, suddenly, he wrenched my left arm up behind my back. Pain surged through me. I gasped and stopped struggling.

"That's better," a gravelly voice said. "Now tell your boyfriend to hand over those coins. He knows what to do with them. Tell him if he doesn't hand them over, someone will get hurt. You got that?"

He jerked my left arm farther upward. I almost passed out from the pain.

"And just so he knows we're serious . . ."

He shoved me and I cried out. I crashed into some garbage cans and fell. As I hit the ground, I heard a sickening crunch. A searing pain shot up my arm. Everything went black for a moment. When my vision cleared, my attacker was gone.

I struggled to my knees and felt the chill from the snow seeping into my joints. I slowly shrugged out of my backpack and almost passed out again from the pain. With my right hand, I opened it and fumbled inside for my cell phone.

It rang before I could punch in any numbers.

"Hey, Robyn." It was Ben. "I was wondering if you wanted me to pick you up. That way—"

"Someone attacked me," I said. "I think my arm is broken."

"What? Where are you?"

I told him. I said, "Call 9-1-1, Ben. Do it now."

.   .   .

They told me later that it was only three minutes from the time I ended my call with Ben to the time the ambulance arrived, but it seemed a lot longer. A police cruiser showed up a few seconds later.

At the hospital, they X-rayed my arm and told me that the doctor would be with me soon. While I waited, one police officer went to call my father. A second officer stayed with me.

"Can you tell me exactly what happened?" he said.

"I was waiting for the bus. Someone grabbed me and dragged me into an alley. I tried to get away from him, but he twisted my arm and then pushed me." I was still shaking. I could still hear the crunch my arm had made when I'd landed. "I didn't know what he was going to do." I squeezed my eyes shut to keep back the tears.

The officer waited for a moment before asking, "Did you get a look at the person who attacked you?"

I shook my head. "It was dark. He grabbed me from behind."

"Can you tell me anything about him—anything at all?"

"He had a deep voice. And he was strong."

"Did you see what he was wearing—maybe when he made his escape?"

"No." Wait. That wasn't completely true. "Gloves. He was wearing dark gloves. I think they were leather."

"Did you notice anything else about him? Anything else he was wearing?"

"No."

"Could you tell if he was tall or short?"

"He was taller than me." Or maybe he just seemed bigger because he was so much stronger than me.

"You say he had a deep voice. What did he say?"

I hesitated. The man who attacked me made it clear that he wanted me to deliver a message. He wanted the coins, and he'd said that Nick knew what to do with them. So for some reason, he believed that Nick had Mr. Schuster's coins. But if I told the police what he had said, wouldn't it just confirm what they already believed—that Nick really had stolen the coins? I decided to keep that part of the story to myself, at least until I had had a chance to talk to Nick again.

"He told me to be quiet," I said instead.

"Did you recognize his voice? Did it sound familiar?"

"No."

"What happened after he told you to be quiet?"

"I tried to get away from him, and he pushed me down." I couldn't help myself. My eyes filled with tears again. The cop handed me another tissue.

"I know this is difficult," he said. "But I have a few more questions, okay?"

I nodded.

"The man who attacked you, did he try anything?"

"No."

"Did he try to make you go with him?"

"No."

"What did he do after he pushed you down?"

"He left."

The officer frowned. "Did something scare him off?"

"I don't know."

"He just pulled you down the alley, pushed you down, and then left? He didn't try to force you to go with him?"

"No."

I could see he wasn't satisfied with my answer.

"Can you think of any reason why someone would want to hurt you?" he said. "Has anyone threatened you? Any trouble at school? Maybe with a boyfriend or former boyfriend?"

"No."

The curtains parted, and the other police officer came in, followed by a doctor and a nurse.

The police officer said, "Your father is on his way here."

"In the meantime, we're going to set that arm," the doctor said.

When they had finished, my arm was in a cast up past my elbow. It was still throbbing. After the doctor left, the nurse said, "There's a young man waiting outside for you. Do you want to see him?"

"Yes, please," I said.

Ben's face was pale with worry and concern. I had forgotten all about him.

"Robyn, are you okay?" he said. He took my right hand in his. "Okay, stupid question." He looked at my cast and sling. "You must have been terrified."

Just like that, it all came out. I started to sob this time. I'd thought the man was going to really hurt me. And when I remembered that voice rumbling in my ear . . .

Ben hugged me, taking care not to hurt my arm.

"You're safe now," he said. He was still holding me when the curtains parted and my father stepped into the cubicle. He wasn't alone.

Nick was with him.

"Robbie, are you all right?" my father said. Ben stepped back from the bed to let him pass. My father held me gently by the shoulders. "They said a man attacked you and dragged you into an alley."

I nodded.

"What happened?"

"I'd just taken Orion back to Elliot Schuster and—"

I glanced at Nick. He'd been staring at Ben, but he looked with surprise at me. My father looked at both boys.

"I don't believe you two know each other," he said. "Ben, this is Nick D'Angelo. Nick, Ben Logan." Ben stiffened at the mention of Nick's name, but he thrust out a hand. After a moment's hesitation, Nick took it. "Now if you two don't mind, I'd like to talk to Robyn alone for a minute."

Nick left first. Ben followed, walking stiffly. He didn't even glance at me.

My dad inspected me and engulfed me in a giant but gentle bear hug. When he finally released me, he said, "Where exactly did this happen, Robbie?"

"A couple of blocks from Mr. Schuster's house," I said. "Dad, why is Nick with you?"

"First things first. You'd just dropped off the dog and then . . . ?"

"Then I went to catch the bus. I was supposed to meet Ben downtown."

"Tell me exactly what happened."

I hesitated. Should I tell him the truth? If it didn't match what the police had already told him, he would notice right away. He would insist that I talk to them again and tell them everything. He believed in being honest with the police and telling them everything so that they could do their job. But I couldn't help but think that in this case, telling them everything would only hurt Nick. I wasn't prepared to do that—at least not until I gave him a chance to explain. I drew in a deep breath and told my dad the same thing I had told the police. He frowned through the whole story.

"Why is Nick with you, Dad?"

"Huh? Oh. There's something I should have told you yesterday, Robbie."

"Yesterday?"

He pulled a chair up beside the bed and sat down facing me. "Nick called me after he was arrested at the mall."

"What? Why?"

"He was afraid to call his aunt. He knows he shouldn't have gone there, but he said he couldn't say no when Isobel told him that Mr. Schuster wanted to see him. All Isobel knew was that her parents wouldn't allow Nick in the house. She didn't know about his bail conditions."

"Nick called *you*?"

"He didn't have a lot of options, Robbie."

"Wait a minute." It was slowly making sense. "Nick told you that someone pushed him, didn't he? That's why you didn't argue with me when I asked if you could talk to mall security and see if there was anything on their cameras. You would have checked it out yourself."

"It was a good idea no matter whose it was. And the reason I didn't tell you was because Nick asked me not to. And because I know how you feel about him now that you're with Ben."

I'm sure he *thought* he knew how I felt.

"I took a copy of the security footage to Nick's lawyer right after I left you," my father said. "He contacted the police. It's obvious Nick didn't push Schuster on purpose. They dropped that charge. But the charges of burglary and breaking-and-entering charges and for the assault on Claudia Schuster still stand. Then there's the matter of his bail conditions, which he clearly breached."

"If he broke bail, why did they release him?" I said.

"The police spoke to Isobel. She confirmed that Mr. Schuster had asked to see Nick and that was the only reason Nick was there. Even so, it took a lot of persuading. I'd already rounded up some people to write letters on Nick's behalf. Those helped. The judge agreed to release him to me."

"To you?" I stared at my father. "You mean he's staying at your place?"

"For the time being. His aunt is furious with him for lying to her. She doesn't want him back in her house. I'm hoping she'll change her mind, but in the meantime, he has nowhere else to go. I know this is awkward, Robbie—"

"Mom's out of town for another whole week. What am I supposed to do?"

"He's going to sleep in my office," my dad said. "He has to report to his youth worker once a week, keep me apprised of his whereabouts at all times, and do exactly what I tell him. If he breaks any of those conditions, they'll lock him up until his case goes to court." He reached for my coat and helped me into it as best he could.

As we left the cubicle, we found Ben and Nick standing on opposite sides of the hall, waiting for us. Ben was staring at Nick. Nick was staring at the floor. Ben started toward me.

"We'll be waiting at the main door," my dad said. He nodded to Nick, who refused to look at me. He followed my father down the hall.

As soon as they were out of sight, Ben said, "So that's the guy you used to go out with?"

I nodded.

"He seems pretty tight with your dad."

"He's in trouble. My dad's helping him out."

"What kind of trouble?"

"It's complicated."

"How is your father helping him out?"

I hesitated. "Nick is staying at my dad's place for a while."

Ben looked at me for what seemed like an eternity.

"Aren't you staying with your father while your mom is out of town?" he said.

"Yes, but—"

"So you and your ex-boyfriend are staying together at your dad's place?"

"It's not what you think—"

"How long has he been staying there?"

"My dad just bailed him out this afternoon."

"Bailed him out? You mean he was arrested?" He frowned as if he was trying to make a difficult decision. "You said you had just finished walking Orion."

"So?"

"There was a dog named Orion at that animal shelter where you volunteered last summer," he said. "Nick trained him, didn't he?"

I stared at him. "How do you know that?" I had avoided giving Ben any details about Nick. I didn't think that they would ever meet, and besides, thinking about Nick always made me feel either angry or sad.

"Morgan told me," he said.

"Why would Morgan tell you that?"

"Because I asked her."

"You asked Morgan about Nick?"

His eyes shifted away from mine.

"Why did you do that?" I said.

His face was defiant when he looked at me again. "Because I wanted to know."

"Know what?"

"Don't look at me like that, Robyn. I didn't commit a crime. I just wanted to know something about the guy who seemed so important to you."

"If you wanted to know, you should have asked *me*."

"If I had asked, would you have told me?"

It was my turn to feel uncomfortable. I looked away.

"I thought so," Ben said.

"I'm sorry," I said, though I was mostly sorry that we were having the conversation. "I wasn't trying to hide anything from you, but—"

"—but you were walking Nick's dog before you were attacked."

"Orion isn't Nick's dog. Nick trained him, but he belongs to someone else."

"Then why were you walking him?"

"I was just helping out a friend."

"Nick?"

"No. I was doing a favor for the dog's owner." I was getting angry.

"Are you still in love with him, Robyn?"

Ben looked deep into my eyes. Maybe he thought if he looked hard enough, he would see what was in my heart.

"My arm hurts," I said. "And my dad is waiting. I have to go."

For a moment, Ben's eyes were sharp and cold. Then his expression softened just a little. He slipped an arm around my waist.

"I'll walk you out," he said.

My dad and Nick were sitting on a bench in the hospital's busy main lobby. They both got to their feet when they saw me. Ben walked me to where they were standing, then leaned over to kiss me. But it didn't seem right, not in front of Nick. I pulled away from him. Ben looked hurt, but all he said was, "I'll call you." He nodded politely to my father and stepped into the revolving doors.

He drove past us a few minutes later, while we were on our way to my dad's car.

"Here we go," my dad said, unlocking his own car. Nick slid into the back seat. No one said a word the whole way to my dad's place.

.   .   .

My father's loft is mostly open concept. Even if Nick slept in the office, I was going to have a hard time avoiding him.

"The couch doesn't pull out," my father said as he showed Nick where to put his things—a backpack and a small duffel bag. "You get settled and I'll get started on dinner. It's late. You two must be hungry. I know I am."

"Do you need any help?" Nick and I said in unison. I had asked so that I'd have an excuse to get away from Nick. Nick had probably asked to get away from me.

"I think I can handle it," my dad said. "You two relax. Watch some TV." He disappeared into the kitchen.

Nick ducked into my father's office and closed the door. I went to my room and sat down on the bed, cradling my broken arm. I wished Nick weren't there—at least, that's what I told myself. I wished my dad hadn't decided to help him—at least, that's what I told myself.

But if I were being honest with myself, neither was true.

What I really wished was that Nick hadn't disappeared three months ago. I wished that he'd stayed in town and that we had stayed together. I had the feeling that if he hadn't left, things would be different. Or would they? Nick would still have been walking Orion for Mr. Schuster. He would still have met Elliot Schuster, who probably would still have fired him. And the coins? They would probably still be missing. And maybe Nick would still have been arrested for stealing them. But I would have known about it sooner. I could have helped him.

I shook my head. What was the matter with me? We weren't still together. I was with Ben—who was angry with me. Which reminded me . . .

I dug my phone out of my backpack and called Morgan's number.

"You just had to tell him, didn't you?" I said.

"What? Robyn, is that you?"

"You told Ben how I met Nick! It sounds like you gave him a full play-by-play."

"Oh," Morgan said. She sounded almost contrite.

"So you did tell him."

"Well, I guess I kind of—"

"Why?"

"Because he asked. I'm sorry, Robyn. But it was a while ago—before Nick came back. I didn't think it mattered." There was a brief pause. "I also didn't think he'd tell you."

"Well, he did."

"Sorry," she murmured again. I relented a little. Morgan was my friend. I knew she wouldn't have said anything to Ben if she'd thought it would hurt me.

"It gets worse," I said. "Ben was at the hospital with me when my dad got there—"

"You were at the hospital? What happened? Did Mr. Schuster get worse? Oh God, he didn't die, did he?"

"I was at a different hospital. The thing is, my dad brought Nick with him."

"He brought Nick to the hospital? Is he okay?"

"He's fine. Someone attacked me."

"Attacked you? What do you mean?"

"I mean, dragged me down a dark alley and threatened me. My arm is broken."

"Okay," Morgan said. "Back up and tell me this story in chronological order, or I'm hanging up and coming over there."

I took a deep breath and told her what had happened from the time I had dropped off Orion to the time I left the hospital.

"Someone attacked you and threatened you and you're mad at me for answering a few of Ben's questions two months ago?" Morgan said. "I don't think you have your priorities straight."

She was right. Just seeing Nick again had turned my whole world upside down.

"I'm sorry," I said. "But you should have seen the look on Ben's face when he found out that Nick is staying here."

"Whoa! Nick is staying at your dad's? But *you're* staying at your dad's place."

"You sound just like Ben."

"I bet."

"Let me get this straight, Robyn. Your current boyfriend is mad because you and your *ex*-boyfriend are living in the same place—and this surprises you?" There was a pause. "It is still ex-boyfriend, isn't it?"

"You were at his aunt's house, Morgan. You saw what he was like."

"Things can change, Robyn."

"Well, they haven't. He and my dad walked in while Ben was hugging me."

There were a few more seconds of silence before Morgan said, "Does Ben have anything to worry about?"

Was there any chance I would get back together with Nick? No—not if Nick had anything to do with it. But what if things were different? What if Nick wanted me back? I was supposed to be with Ben, but I couldn't get Nick out of my mind.

"Does he, Robyn?"

"I guess not."

"So talk to Ben. He'll forgive you."

"Forgive me? I didn't do anything wrong."

"Except get involved in Nick's problems without telling him. And see Nick without mentioning it to him. And . . ."

"I get it," I said.

CHAPTER **THIRTEEN**

My dad whipped up omelets and toast. He ate heartily. I picked at the food on my plate. So did Nick. He stared at the table the whole time. I told myself I didn't care. My arm was throbbing.

"Well, this is fun," my dad said.

I gave him a warning look. The rest of the meal passed in silence. My father frowned slightly as he ate, chewing over a problem.

As soon as we finished eating, Nick volunteered to clean up. My dad accepted his offer.

"Come on, Robbie," he said. "We need to talk."

I followed him into the living room and sank down on one of his comfy sofas. My dad brought along a small bottle of painkillers and handed me a tablet.

"You can take another one in six hours if you need to," he said. He leaned forward to look at me. "Robbie, I need you to tell me again what happened."

I repeated what I had already told him—and the police—at the hospital.

"Do you remember anything else about the man who attacked you? Anything at all?" he said.

I shook my head. I hadn't seen anything except his gloves.

"So you were waiting for the bus, and this man came up behind you and grabbed you, is that right?"

"He put a hand over my mouth, told me not to scream, and dragged me down an alley beside a store. When I struggled, he twisted my arm. I thought he was going to dislocate my shoulder. Then he pushed me and I fell."

My dad frowned, just as he had at the hospital. "Did he say anything first? Threaten you in any way?"

I don't like to lie to my dad. I hardly ever do it. But I knew what he would do if I told him the truth: make me tell the police. I just needed a little more time. I needed to hear Nick's side of the story. I owed him that.

"It doesn't make sense," my father said. "Why did he grab you? "Robbie, this man didn't . . . he didn't try to get you to go with him, did he?"

Police officers and ex-police officers—they all think alike.

"No, nothing like that. He just grabbed me, that's all. Maybe he was crazy."

My dad's frown deepened. "It's not like you were in a dangerous neighborhood."

"You're always telling me to be aware of my surroundings, that crime doesn't just happen in poor areas."

"True." He looked at the cast on my arm. "Your mother's going to have a fit when she hears what happened."

I wasn't looking forward to telling her, but there was no way to avoid it. My arm wouldn't be healed by the time she and Ted returned from their vacation.

"You sure there isn't anything else you can tell me about what happened, Robbie?"

"I'm sure. I'm going to try to get some sleep, Dad."

He nodded. "That's probably a good idea."

I passed the kitchen on the way to my room, where Nick was wiping off the counter. I wondered if he'd overheard our conversation.

.   .   .

I lay on my bed, staring at the ceiling. The painkiller my father had given me was kicking in. The throbbing in my arm started to ease. But my brain was racing. The man who had attacked me believed that Nick had the missing coins. He'd threatened me because he wanted me to deliver a message to Nick. The more I thought about it, the more questions I had.

My attacker knew that I knew Nick. But except for two short visits to his aunt's house, I hadn't been anywhere near Nick in three months. Had the guy been following me? Or had someone told him that I knew Nick?

And what made my attacker so sure Nick had the coins? I thought about what the man had said—tell him to hand them over. Over to whom? And the really big question: what could—or should—I do about it?

I waited until the loft was silent, then got up and crept into my dad's office.

I nearly jumped out of my skin when the room filled with light. Nick sat up, his hand on the switch of the lamp beside the couch. He was wearing a pair of old sweatpants and a T-shirt. His hair, still too long, was disheveled. His purple-blue eyes burned into mine.

"What are you doing in here?" he said.

"We have to talk."

The look on his face was one of purposeful indifference—Nick telling me that he didn't care about me or anything to do with me.

"Your boyfriend has a nice car," he said. "Let me guess. He's loaded, right?"

"His family is well off, if that's what you mean."

He looked down at my hand. "Nice ring too," he said. "How much do you figure that set him back?"

"I didn't ask."

"Of course not. That wouldn't be polite, would it?" He switched off the light. I heard him settle back down on the couch.

"The man who attacked me," I said quietly into the darkness, "he told me to give you a message."

For a moment it was silent in the room. Then the room filled with light again. Nick peered at me.

"What message?"

"He grabbed me, Nick. He put a hand over my mouth so I couldn't scream. Then he wrenched my arm back and said, 'Tell your boyfriend to hand over the coins.' He said you knew what to do with them. He said if you didn't . . . " I shuddered as I remembered his words.

"If I didn't, what?"

"Someone would get hurt."

"Why didn't you tell your dad that?"

So he had been listening to us. "The police think you stole those coins. So does Mr. Schuster's family. If I told the police what that man said, it would only make them more convinced that you did it. I wanted to talk to you first. I want to know what's going on."

"The guy your dad saw on the security video," Nick said. "The one who slammed into me. I think he could be the same guy who hurt you."

"What makes you say that?"

"Right after I met up with Mr. Schuster and Isobel, someone tapped me on the shoulder. I started to turn around to see what the problem was. A man whispered in my ear. He said if I didn't deliver the coins, someone was going to pay."

"Deliver them?"

"He told me where to take them."

"Where?"

"What difference does it make?"

Was he kidding? "We could leave them there—"

Nick's eyes drilled into mine. "I don't have the coins, Robyn."

"Nick, if you took them for any reason, maybe to keep them safe from Elliot—"

"I didn't. I'm really sorry about what happened to Mr. Schuster and to you, but I don't know why that man thinks I have those coins. I never touched them."

Now that we were face-to-face, now that I was looking into his eyes, I knew he was telling me the truth.

"I'm sorry. I thought—"

"I know what you thought."

I was pretty sure he didn't, but I didn't think he would believe me if I told him.

"As long as he thinks you have them, maybe we can find out who he is," I said. "We could leave a package where he said. Then we could watch and see who picks it up, see if it's the same person who attacked me and pushed you."

"But you told your dad you didn't see the guy."

"I didn't. But you did, on the escalator."

He shook his head. "I started to turn around, but he told me not to. He told me to listen. I didn't get a look at him. And I saw that security video from the mall. You can't see the guy's face or his hair or anything. You can't even tell he was talking to me."

"Still," I said, "if we drop off the coins and someone picks them up, that has to prove something."

"Right," he said. "We drop a package that doesn't contain the stolen coins in a garbage can—"

"A garbage can?"

"That's what he said. It's a garbage can in the park. And some guy picks it up and, if anyone asks him, claims he was just picking through the garbage or something and found a package that doesn't even contain any coins. What will that prove?"

I hated to admit it, but he was right. We wouldn't be any further ahead. And if we told the police why we were doing it, it could make things worse for Nick.

"Why did he push you, Nick?"

"He said he wanted me to understand that he was serious about what he was saying."

"My attacker said the same thing. And you have no idea who he was?"

"None."

"How would he have known you'd be at the mall? Were you followed? Have you noticed anyone hanging around your aunt's house?"

He shook his head.

"Did you tell the police what he said?"

"What do you think, Robyn?"

I sat down on the couch next to him.

"Nick, I need you to be honest with me."

He stiffened a little. "I've always been honest with you."

"That's not how I remember it."

"Okay, maybe we got off to a bad start. But after what happened in Chinatown, I promised myself—no more lies. Not to you."

I was sitting so close to him that I could feel his breath on my neck. I ached to touch him.

"Nick, how did some of the coins end up in your backpack?"

I thought he would get angry, but he didn't. "I don't know," he said.

I searched his eyes. He didn't blink or look away.

"I believe you," I said. I hesitated to ask more questions, but I had to know. "Someone saw you lurking around Mr. Schuster's house the day the coins were stolen . . ."

"I wasn't lurking. I wanted to see if Orion was okay."

"My dad says you also don't have an alibi for when it happened. Where were you the night of the break-in?"

His eyes shifted to the floor.

"You said no more lies, Nick."

He got up and walked to the door. For a moment I thought he was going to walk out. Instead, he pointed up—to the skylight above the dining area.

"I was up there," he said.

"You were on the roof?"

He nodded.

"What were you doing up there?"

"You were sitting at the table practically the whole night with your computer," he said softly. "For a while, you were on the Internet. It looked like maybe you were researching an assignment. After that, you did a lot of typing. Then you pulled a book out of your backpack and just kind of zoned out. I couldn't tell what you were reading—the way you were sitting, your head was in the way. But I noticed you didn't turn any pages."

My cheeks burned. Ben had been at a family dinner that night. Billy and Morgan were out. So I'd spent a Friday night doing my homework—well, doing some homework. When Nick had seen me looking at that book, I hadn't been reading. I'd been staring at a photograph—of Nick and me.

"You were watching me that night?" I said.

"A couple of other nights too."

"Why?"

He shifted uneasily but didn't answer.

"We should tell my dad," I said. "And the police. You couldn't have robbed Mr. Schuster if you were up on the roof all that time."

He turned and went back to the couch where he'd been sleeping. What was the matter with him?

"Don't you get it, Nick? You do have an alibi. They'll have to believe you."

"What alibi?" he said. "I have an ex-girlfriend who didn't even see me that night. The same ex-girlfriend who's up to her eyeballs in this thing. She's come to see me a couple of times. She's been walking Mr. Schuster's dog. She was at the mall when I supposedly pushed Mr. Schuster. And as soon as her dad bails me out, she suddenly comes forward and says she was doing exactly what I described her doing that night." He shook his head. "If I was a cop, I wouldn't believe it. I'd think that you were lying to help me. Wouldn't you?"

"But if you're telling the truth . . ."

"They won't believe me. And they won't believe you."

He was right again, as much as I didn't want to admit it. I wished I had looked up that night. I wished I'd seen him.

"My dad will believe me," I said.

Nick made a face. "If it's all the same to you, I'd rather he didn't know. It's not going to convince the cops I'm innocent, and it will only make your dad think I'm some kind of stalker."

"But—"

"Please, Robyn. He's been good to me. I don't want to jeopardize that."

Reluctantly, I agreed—for the time being.

"That doesn't change the fact that I know what I was doing that night and that you couldn't have described it if you hadn't seen me." If I'd had any doubts left, they were all gone. There was no way Nick had anything to do with Mr. Schuster's missing coin collection.

Nick was silent for a minute. "Robyn?" His voice was soft again. "Is it serious with that guy?"

"You mean Ben?"

He winced at the name.

"Why did you wait so long to call me, Nick?" It had taken him nearly two months. He had left me a garbled voice mail message. I hadn't been able to make out a phone number where I could reach him. "And why didn't you call me back after you left that message?"

"You know how it is. Stuff happens. Things didn't work out the way I expected. At first I couldn't call you. Then—" He shrugged. "Then I didn't want to."

"Thanks a lot," I muttered. I turned for the door. Nick grabbed my hand to stop me. It was the first time he'd touched me since he'd disappeared. He looked at me for a moment. Then he dropped my hand.

"I ran into a little trouble," he said. "But I didn't want to tell you because I didn't want you to think I was a total screw-up. I thought I'd sort things out and call when I was in the clear. I guess I should have known it wasn't going to work out when you didn't even try to get in touch with me—"

"Get in touch with you?"

"Then I left you that message, and you still didn't call back. I should have figured you'd found someone else. I mean, why wouldn't you?" He shook his head. "I must have been crazy to think you'd want to be with me. I saw you with that guy, Robyn. I saw him put that ring on your finger."

"I *did* call you back," I said. "At least, I tried. I tried the number you called from. But it was a pay phone. I couldn't get through."

"You were supposed to leave me a message at Beej's."

"I couldn't hear you. Your voice was drowned out by all the noise in the background. Where were you calling from, anyway?"

"One of those gas station-restaurant places on the highway."

"Why didn't you call me again? I kept waiting for you to."

He looked skeptically at me. "Are you trying to tell me that you only started going out with that guy after I left you that message? How dumb do I look? You expect me to believe that just because I didn't call again, you went out and found someone else and that just a couple of days after that, he's giving you an expensive ring?" He drew in a deep breath. "I'm sorry," he said. "I have no right to be angry. You look good with that guy, Robyn. You two look like you belong together. And I bet your mom likes him, huh?"

"Nick—"

"Look, I'm sorry I got your dad involved in this. But I didn't know who else to call. My aunt is pissed off because I violated my bail conditions. She doesn't want me back if I can't obey the rules. Your dad said he'd help me find a good lawyer and get the charges dealt with as fast as possible. After that, I'll be out of your life. I promise." He sunk into the couch and turned off the light.

I reached out and touched his arm. He laid a hand over mine for a moment and then gently brushed me away.

"Being here is hard enough, Robyn," he said. "Don't make it any harder, okay?"

CHAPTER FOURTEEN

I woke up with a start and could just make out a large, shadowy figure creeping toward my bed in the dark. I shot up, my heart pounding.

"Sorry, Robbie," said a soft voice. "I didn't mean to wake you."

I reached out and switched on the lamp on my bedside table. "Dad, what are you doing?" I glanced at the clock. It was five in the morning, but he was fully dressed. "Is something wrong?"

"No. I just need to get something." He crossed to the closet that ran along one wall of my room and opened it. I got a chill when he bent down in front of a big metal lockbox on the floor—it was where he kept his gun. But to my relief, he picked up a briefcase instead and dusted it off.

"I need to talk to you about something, Dad."

"I'm afraid it's going to have to wait. I'm in kind of a hurry."

"Are you going somewhere?"

"Something came up. I left you a note. I should be back sometime tomorrow. We'll talk then, okay?"

"Okay."

He slid the closet door shut. "When Nick gets up, I want the two of you to go over to Henri's. Tell Nick he's to stay there until I get back. Tell him I mean it, Robbie."

Henri (short for Henrietta) is Vernon Deloitte's girl-friend. Vern is my father's business partner.

"Nick would never leave here, if that's what you're worried about, Dad. He'd never do anything to make you mad at him."

"That's good to know—but that's not what I'm worried about. Someone has to be responsible for him, and I can't do that if I'm not here."

"I'll be responsible for him."

"You're not old enough, Robbie. And after what happened"—he looked pointedly at the cast on my arm—"I'd feel a whole lot better if you were somewhere safe. Not to mention what would happen if your mother ever found out that I left you and Nick here alone . . . " He shook his head. "Go along with me on this. Nick stays put at Henri's, and both of you stay over there tonight. Okay?"

"Okay."

After my dad left, I couldn't get back to sleep. I crept into the living room, put the TV on at low volume, and dozed off soon afterward.

. . .

I woke up a couple of hours later when the door to my father's office opened. Nick looked out, a bland expression on his face.

"I'm going to go and clean up," he said.

I was still curled up in the same chair by the time Nick had showered and changed into jeans and a fresh T-shirt. His hair was still damp. I told him what my father had said. He shrugged and said okay.

"Mind if I get something to eat first?" he said.

"Go ahead." As he padded over to the kitchen in his sock feet, I called after him. "In the DVD Beej gave me, you said that you were asleep on Mr. Schuster's couch when Elliot and his family showed up."

Nick turned slowly to look at me. "I'd been staying in an abandoned building," he said. "I didn't think Mr. Schuster would mind if I bunked at his place while he was in the hospital. Someone had to look after Orion."

"How did you get into the house?"

"I used my key."

"You have a key to Mr. Schuster's house?"

Nick frowned. "You sound surprised."

"I'm sorry. I didn't mean—"

"Mr. Schuster trusted me. He gave me a key to the front door, one to the side door. You know, in case he was at a doctor's appointment or something when I came over to walk Orion."

"Did you tell the police you had keys?"

"Have," he said. "I still have them. What's with all the questions, Robyn?"

"I'm trying to figure out what happened."

His expression soured. "So now you don't believe me?"

"I do believe you," I said. "That's why I'm trying to figure it out. Come on, Nick. Did you tell the police you have keys to Mr. Schuster's house?"

He shook his head.

"Why not?" I said. "They said that the person who took the coins broke into the house. But you didn't have to break in. You have keys."

"Most cops I've ever met, once they tag you as a screw-up, they can't see you any other way, ever," Nick said, his voice heavy with disdain. "If I told them I had keys, they'd think I used a crowbar just to throw them off." When I looked skeptical, he said, "Think about it, Robyn. It's not like Mr. Schuster gives out house keys to the whole world. If the coins were stolen but there was no sign of forced entry, someone with a key must have taken them. So if I used a key, it would be like pointing the finger at myself. But if I used a crowbar, I could say it wasn't me, I didn't need to break in, I had a key. That's the way the cops would see it, Robyn. Guaranteed."

"You went back to Mr. Schuster's house after you were released on the breaking-and-entering charge. Why?"

He looked intently at me for a moment, trying to decide how much to say.

"I wanted to talk to Mr. Schuster," he said at last. "I went to the hospital first. But they said he'd been discharged."

"What did you want to talk to him about?"

"What do you think?" His voice edged with frustration. "I wanted to tell him I would never steal from him."

"What happened when you got to the house?"

He sighed, came over to where I was sitting, and sank into a chair opposite me.

"I was hoping Elliot wouldn't be there. He's a scary guy when he's mad. When his wife answered the door, I thought it was going to be okay. At least she knew me. She knew what Mr. Schuster thought about me too. I thought for sure she'd let me talk to him."

Nick had said to Beej that when Elliot found him in the house that first day, he'd thought Claudia would say something. I thought he'd meant that he thought Claudia would calm Elliot down. But that didn't seem to be it.

"She knew you? You mean you'd met Claudia before?"

"Yeah. I didn't know her well or anything. But she dropped by one time last fall when I was at the house."

"Isobel told me that they haven't visited Mr. Schuster in years." Then I remembered what Schuster's neighbor Esther had said: Elliot hadn't visited his father since his mother had died, but Claudia had.

"I know. Mr. Schuster told me. I guess that's why he was so surprised when she showed up. She said she was in town for some kind of convention. I could tell she was wondering what I was doing there. Anyway, we talked. Mr. Schuster told her about the program I was in while

I was at the animal shelter." He shifted uncomfortably in his chair. "Mr. Schuster always tells me I have nothing to be ashamed of. He says I've changed—that if anything, I should be proud of myself. But . . ."

"He's right," I said quietly.

He brightened for a moment. Then his eyes went to my ring. I slid my hand out of sight.

"Anyway," he continued, "I assumed that she would have told Elliot about me. But I guess she didn't, because when Elliot fired me, he acted like I'd been lying to him, hiding my past. But I wasn't. I really thought he knew. You should have seen him, Robyn. He got all red in the face and started yelling. He said he'd had me checked out. He said he didn't want a criminal anywhere near his father's house."

I thought back to what Nick had said on the DVD: the coins disappeared a few days later.

"After they released me on the breaking and entering, I went back to the house. I wanted to set things straight with Mr. Schuster. Claudia was there alone, but she wouldn't let me in. Then I heard Orion barking down in the basement. The basement, Robyn! I wanted to get him out of there, but Claudia wouldn't let me do that, either. I'd already told them about the basement—"

"What's so important about the basement?" I said.

"When Mr. Schuster adopted Orion, he set up his bed in the basement. That's where all his other dogs used to sleep—his wife used to insist on it, and he kind of got into the habit. But it was nice, you know? He had it fixed up with a blanket and a basket and a nice big pillow. Really cozy. But Orion didn't like it down there. Mr. Schuster couldn't figure out why. Then, before I left town, he told me that he'd found out that Orion's original owner—the one that abandoned him—used to keep Orion locked in the basement for months at a time. No exercise, no sunshine, just a dark unfinished basement. So Mr. Schuster moved his bed upstairs to his coin room."

"Coin room?"

"It's really a spare bedroom at the back of the house, but Mr. Schuster called it the coin room because it's where he kept his coin collection."

"And that's where Orion was the night the Schusters arrived and he bit Claudia?" I said.

"It was just a nip," Nick said. "She must have known he was in there. He was barking. But she barged in on him anyway. He can be a little territorial. Anyway, when I went to set things straight with Mr. Schuster and I heard Orion down in the basement, I had to do something. I had to get him out of there."

"Claudia says you forced your way into the house."

He hung his head. "Maybe I lost my temper. The next thing I knew, Claudia was calling the cops." He let out a long sigh. "I was in enough trouble. I didn't need any more. So I left."

I hated to ask the next question, but I had to be sure. "Did you hit her, Nick?"

"No way. I didn't touch her."

"She told the police you did."

"She lied," he said bitterly. "But the cops arrested me again. When they released me that time, they told me I had to stay away from Mr. Schuster, his house, and his family."

"Isobel told me that Mr. Schuster and Elliot hardly ever spoke to each other. She said that the family hadn't seen Mr. Schuster since before his wife died. She and Connor kept in touch with him by e-mail. But she never mentioned that her mother had visited him."

"Yeah, well, I could see why she might not want to tell the kids," Nick said.

"What do you mean?"

"Mr. Schuster told me that the real reason she showed up was to ask for money."

"He actually said that?"

"Yeah. He was pretty mad about it. Claudia told him that Elliot's business was in trouble."

"He owes a lot of money," I said.

"It doesn't surprise me," Nick said. "Elliot's all about money, according to Mr. Schuster. He told me that the only time he'd heard from him recently was when Elliot called to bug him about insuring his coin collection. Mr. Schuster was pretty surprised about that too. He always said that the only difference Elliot could see between an 1850 and an 1851 Seated Liberty Silver Dollar was the date."

"Is there another difference?"

"Sure is. One's worth a couple of hundred dollars. The other is worth a couple of thousand. But Elliot didn't know that. He didn't know anything about coins."

"Until Connor told him," I said.

Nick digested that piece of information. "Maybe that's why Elliot suddenly wanted Mr. Schuster to get his collection insured. He arranged the whole thing, you know. Mr. Schuster only went along with it because he wanted to make sure that if anything happened, his grandson would be able to collect. He said he probably should have had them insured a long time ago. But Mr. Schuster didn't collect those coins because of what they were worth. He collected them because he loved them. He'd pick one up and start talking about it—it would be like a history lesson, you know?" He smiled. "Mr. Schuster said he'd loved to have seen the look on Elliot's face when he found out that Connor was going to inherit the bulk of the collection."

"What do you mean, the bulk of it? Isobel told me that Connor was going to inherit the whole collection."

Nick hesitated. "Mr. Schuster said he was going to leave some coins to me."

"He did?"

"He said he'd even decided which ones but that he wasn't going to tell me. It was going to be a surprise." He shook his head. "He liked to talk about coins and history and stuff like that. It made him happy, so I listened. I think he got the idea I was as interested as he was."

"Are you?"

"The history part of it is okay. But I know his grandson is really into coins. He should get them all. He'd appreciate them way more than I would. I tried to tell

Mr. Schuster that. I told him if he wanted to leave me something, he could leave me Orion. You know what he said?"

I raised my eyebrows.

"He said if I kept going the way I was—in school, with a job, a place to live—he'd consider it. He said he wouldn't let just anyone have Orion. It would have to be someone who could give him a good home. Guess that's not going to happen." He stood up abruptly. "We should get going. I don't want your dad to call Henri and find out we're not there."

"Okay," I said. But there was one thing that was bothering me. One big thing.

CHAPTER **FIFTEEN**

"Coins don't jump into backpacks all by themselves, Nick."

"I thought you said you believed me."

"I do. What I mean is, someone had to have put those coins there," I said. "You have your backpack with you pretty much all the time, don't you?"

He nodded.

"Did you ever see anyone mess with it?"

"No."

"And it's never been out of your sight?"

"No." He hesitated. "Well, almost never."

"What do you mean, 'almost'?"

He looked down at the floor. "I used to stash it whenever I went to the hotel," he said. He spoke so quietly that I wasn't sure I'd heard him correctly.

"Hotel?"

"But I always put it somewhere safe. And when I got

back, it was always right where I'd left it."

"I don't understand," I said. "What hotel?"

"What difference does it make? I'd stash it, I'd be gone for forty-five minutes, an hour at the most, and it was always there when I came back."

"And you never noticed anything different about it?"

He shook his head. "I always just checked to make sure my stuff was still there, and it always was."

If Nick didn't take Mr. Schuster's collection—and I was 100-percent positive that he hadn't—then someone must have put those coins in his backpack. But how? And when?

"I don't understand. Why did you go to a hotel?"

"To clean up, okay?" he said. He sounded angry.

"Clean up?"

"It's bad enough I had to do it," he said. "Now I have to tell you about it?" His eyes burned into me. "There's this big hotel not far from where I was staying. It has these huge bathrooms down where all the conference rooms and meeting rooms are. There's no running water where I was living. So I'd go there to wash up. There's this one time of day when you're guaranteed no one will walk in on you. I tried to look like I worked there, you know, maybe as a janitor or a maintenance guy. Carrying a backpack would have made me look like I didn't belong, so I always stashed it before I went. Satisfied?"

"Why didn't you stay with your aunt?" I asked. "Or come back here? My dad would have let you have your place back." Then he wouldn't have been in Mr. Schuster's house when Elliot and his family had arrived.

The buzzer sounded.

I got up, pressed the intercom button, and said, "Yes?"

"Robyn, it's me." Ben. "I need to talk to you."

I glanced at Nick. He looked away.

"Come on up," I said. As I buzzed him through the downstairs door, I turned back to Nick. "I didn't know he was coming over," I said apologetically.

"I'm going to get my stuff," Nick said. He disappeared into my dad's office.

I heard Ben's footsteps out in the hall and opened the door before he could knock. He was carrying a bouquet of flowers, which he handed to me.

"How's your arm?" he said.

"Sore."

"Then we'll have to find things to do that won't hurt it. We're off all week, Robyn, and I don't want anything to ruin—" His eyes shifted to someplace over my shoulder and his expression changed. I turned and saw Nick, his backpack over his shoulder and his duffel bag in his hand. He stared at Ben.

"I'm going to Henri's," he said. He pulled his jacket out of the closet.

"Wait," I said.

"Robyn—" Ben began.

I pulled away from him.

"Did you go to that hotel at the same time every day?"

"What difference does it make?" Nick said.

"What hotel?" Ben said.

"Please, Nick. Just answer the question."

"Yeah," he said sullenly. "The coast was always clear right around one thirty, after everyone had had their lunch and gone back to their meetings. Sometimes there was no one down there at all."

"Did you go to the hotel the day the coins were stolen?"

"What coins?" Ben said.

"I went every day."

"We have to get in touch with Isobel," I said.

"Who's Isobel?" Ben said. "What's going on?"

"Someone planted stolen property on Nick."

Ben frowned. "I thought you told me that you and he—"

"Ben, he'll go to jail if someone doesn't do something."

Ben didn't say a word. I got the feeling that he wouldn't have minded if Nick got locked up for life.

I reached for the phone. My dad's number was blocked—it wouldn't show up on Mr. Schuster's phone. But what if Elliot or Claudia answered instead of Isobel? Would they recognize my voice?

"Here," I said, thrusting the phone at Ben. "Ask for Isobel. Say you're a friend of hers from school."

"It would be nice to know who Isobel is."

"I'll explain, I promise. Please? It's important."

He didn't look happy, but he nodded. I punched in Mr. Schuster's number and listened as Ben asked if he could please speak to Isobel.

"It's her," he said, holding the phone out to me.

"Isobel? It's me, Robyn."

"Ro—"

I cut her off. "I need to talk to you. Is anyone listening? Just answer yes or no."

"Yes," she said.

"Can you get away from the house to meet me?"

After a slight pause, she said, "Yes."

"That's great . . . Is your grandfather still in the hospital?"

"Yes."

"Are you going to visit him?"

"Yes."

"Can you tell me when? Just say a number."

"One."

"You're going to see him at one today at the hospital?"

"Yes."

"There's a coffee place in the lobby. Can you meet me there for a few minutes at, say, one thirty?"

"Yes."

"Great. Thanks. And Isobel? If anyone asks, say it was a friend from school calling, okay?"

"Okay," she said.

I hung up.

"Why do you want to talk to Isobel?" Nick asked.

"Someone put those coins in your backpack, right?"

"Yeah, but—"

"If a complete stranger broke into the house and stole those coins, why would he plant some of them on you? How would he even know about you, let alone where to find you?"

He thought about that for a moment. "You think the thief was someone who knows Mr. Schuster?"

"And who knows you too," I said.

"A lot of people in the neighborhood know me. I was there every day for a couple of months to walk Orion. Any number of people could have seen me, Robyn." He thought for another moment. "Mr. Schuster had the house painted last fall. I got to know the two guys who did the job. You don't think it could have been them, do you?"

"Do you?" I asked back.

CHAPTER **SIXTEEN**

Ben drove us to Henri's house and waited in the car while I went inside with Nick. Nick and Henri had met last fall. She greeted him warmly.

"I'll be back after I've talked to Isobel," I said.

Nick watched grimly from Henri's front door as Ben and I drove away.

. . .

Isobel was sitting at the back of the crowded coffee shop off the main entrance to the hospital. She looked like she had been crying. Then her eyes went to the cast on my arm.

"What happened?" she said.

"It's a long story," I said. "What's the matter, Isobel? Is your grandfather okay?"

"The doctor was just talking to him. My dad says we can't stay at Grandpa's much longer, and the doctor says

Grandpa shouldn't be living by himself anymore. My dad said Grandpa could come and live with us, but Grandpa said no. So then he said that Grandpa would have to go into a nursing home. Grandpa didn't want to do that, either."

I didn't blame him. I remembered when my father had to put my grandfather into a nursing home. He said that when people go into a home, they have to give up most of the things that they spent a lifetime accumulating— their home, their neighbors . . . their pets.

"What about Orion?"

"That's what Grandpa is most upset about," Isobel said. "He agreed to the nursing home on one condition— my dad has to find a good home for Orion. Otherwise, he won't go. I feel sad for Grandpa. I wish he'd come to live with us instead." She looked at Ben. "Are you the one who called me?"

Ben nodded.

"Are you Robyn's boyfriend?"

Ben looked expectantly at me, waiting for my answer.

"I'm sure Nick didn't steal those coins, Isobel," I said, trying not to notice the hurt expression on Ben's face. "But I can't prove it. That's why I wanted to talk to you. I was hoping you could tell me everything you can remember about what happened."

"I have told you, Robyn."

"Maybe you forgot something," I said. "Can you tell me again?"

She frowned. "There isn't much to tell. We all went out to dinner and when we came back, the coins were gone."

"What about earlier in the day?"

"Earlier? Well, I was home all morning. We all were. Then, around noon, my mom and I came to the hospital, and I spent the rest of the day here with Grandpa. Why?"

"I thought if you were at your grandfather's house, you might have seen something. Or noticed someone lurking around."

"Sorry," she said.

"What about your father?" I asked Isobel. "Was he at the house that afternoon?"

She shook her head. "He left before lunch. He had to go to a meeting out of town. Something about his business."

"Do you know where the meeting was?"

She shook her head. "Only that it was out of town. And that it was the wrong day."

"Wrong day?"

"He said he was almost there when he realized that he'd made a mistake. The meeting wasn't until the next week. He had to turn around and drive all the way home. We were supposed to meet him at the restaurant, but he showed up at Grandpa's house to pick us up."

"Did he go to the meeting the next week?"

Isobel frowned. "I don't think so," she said. "No, he didn't go anywhere. Maybe the meeting was canceled. He hasn't been in a very good mood."

So Elliot had no alibi for most of the day of the robbery. But the coins hadn't been discovered missing until after the family came back from the restaurant.

"What about Connor? Where was he?"

"He went to the big reference library downtown to do some homework. Connor likes libraries. He said he found a nice desk off in the corner."

"And you and your mom were here at the hospital all afternoon."

Isobel shook her head again. "My mom was only here part of the time. She went off to buy a glass to replace one of Grandpa's special glasses that she accidentally broke that morning."

"So she bought the glass, and then she came back to the hospital?"

"She came back to the hospital, but she didn't buy the glass. She said she went to every department store in town, but none of them had the exact same type."

"She must have been gone for a long time," I said.

"She was. Almost three hours."

"After you left the hospital, what happened?"

"Mom and I went back to Grandpa's house. Connor showed up a little while after that. Then my dad showed up. He wanted to take a shower before we went out, but my mom said she was too hungry to wait."

"Then what?"

"Then we went to dinner."

"Do you remember what time?"

"Around seven thirty, when we left the house."

That's what my dad had said. It had been in the police report.

"After dinner, we stopped at a bookstore so Connor could buy a coin magazine. As soon as we got home, Connor and I went up to check if Grandpa had a coin that he'd seen in the magazine. Orion was barking, so my dad went to check on him. That's when he noticed that there was something wrong with the side door—it had been broken open. By then Connor and I had found out the coins were missing. My dad called the police."

"He told them about Nick, didn't he?"

Isobel nodded. "He told them where they could find him too."

"How did he know where Nick was living?"

"I told you. Dad hired someone. He had Nick checked out. Connor and I heard him telling my mom before he fired Nick."

"And he said he knew where Nick was living?"

"He had the address. He said it was an old building?"

I nodded. "But that's not where the police found Nick," I said.

"I know," Isobel said.

I stared at her. "You do?"

"The police came to Grandpa's house after they arrested Nick. They told my dad that Nick wasn't where Dad had said he might be, but they found a crowbar there. They said they found Nick someplace else and that he had some of Grandpa's coins on him. They showed them to my dad. But he didn't know if they were part of Grandpa's coin collection. He had to ask Connor."

"And Connor identified them?"

She nodded. "He said they were Grandpa's. Then my dad found some papers from the insurance company. The coins were listed on it. My dad said it figured that the coins the police found were the least valuable ones in the whole collection."

"Did they say where they'd found Nick?" I asked.

"They said he was staying with a girl. My dad asked if it was the girl who had come to the house with Nick— he described her. The police said yes. And that's all I know. I guess I haven't been very helpful, have I?"

I wasn't sure.

"Robyn?" She looked awkwardly at me. "I'm sorry I told my dad about you and Nick. He was so angry. I tried to tell him how much Grandpa liked Nick and that you were only trying to help."

"It's okay, Isobel," I said. "Tell your grandpa I'll come and see him soon. Tell him I'm thinking about him."

.   .   .

"You don't have to do this," I said when Ben pulled up outside of Henri's house. Henri lives in the heart of the financial district. Her closest neighbors—so close that they rub shoulders with her little house—are downtown office towers.

"I want to," Ben said. "Unless there's some reason you don't want my help."

"But it isn't your problem."

"It isn't *yours*, either." He looked at me for a moment.

"You didn't answer when Isobel asked if I was your boy-friend. Is there something you're not telling me?"

I couldn't meet his eyes. "I'm sorry," I mumbled. "There's just so much going on."

He didn't say anything, but I knew he was disappointed by my answer. He got out of the car, circled around to my side, and opened the door for me.

We found Nick sitting at the big oak table in Henri's dining room, cutting a picture out of the newspaper. A huge stack of old papers sat on the table in front of him. He started to smile when he saw me, but his smile vanished when Ben followed me in.

"Where's Henri?" I said.

"Upstairs." Henri is an artist—a painter. Her studio is on the second floor of her house. I looked at the scissors in Nick's hand and the small pile of photo clippings near his elbow.

"I asked if there was anything I could do," he said. "It's for some new project she's planning."

I pulled out a chair and sat down. Ben sat beside me.

"Nick," I said. "Did you tell Elliot where you were living?"

"Are you kidding?" he said. "That's not something you go around telling everybody."

"But he knew."

Nick shrugged. "Like I said, he hired someone to check me out."

"Were you the only person who slept in that building?"

"I saw six, maybe eight, different guys around at different times. It's a big place. People are always going inside to get in out of the wind or have a few drinks or whatever."

"And where is this place exactly?"

He shook his head. "Uh-uh. No way."

"Come on, Nick."

Ben straightened up. He knew something was going on.

"You're not going down there, Robyn," Nick said.

"Someone put those coins in your backpack without you knowing. The only time anyone could have done that was when you left your bag where you were sleeping and went to the hotel. Maybe one of the other people who hang out there saw something."

"It's too dangerous," Nick said. "Even I was careful down there. But you?"

"I'll go with her," Ben said.

"You're kidding," Nick said. I gave him a sharp look. "Come on, Robyn, look at him. Those jeans could be fresh from the cleaners. He looks like a rookie undercover cop." He stood up. "I'll do it."

"You can't and you know it. My dad agreed to take responsibility for you, and he wants you to stay here. Henri promised him she'd keep you here. And Ben has been volunteering at a homeless shelter for ages. He knows how to talk to people, Nick. He's good at it."

Nick scowled at Ben. He was frustrated, and that made me worry for a moment. But he drew in a few deep breaths and his body unclenched.

"At least take Beej with you," he said. "She's been down there before. She knows her way around. People always talk to Beej."

"Beej?" Ben said.

"She's a friend of Nick's," I said.

I had to admit it was a good idea. Although I had no doubt that Ben could talk to people, Beej could probably relate even better. I pulled out my phone and handed it to Nick. He punched in a number. Beej must have answered because Nick started to explain what he wanted. He told her that Ben and I would pick her up.

"Can I talk to her for a minute?" I said.

He handed me the phone again. When I finished the call, Nick said, "What's going on, Robyn?"

"When I figure that out, you'll be the first to know," I promised.

Nick stood up and got scratch paper and a pencil from the kitchen counter. "Beej knows where the building is," he said as he sketched. "I was staying here." He drew an X in the northwest corner of the building he had drawn. "It's in the basement. It's warmer down there. There were some other guys sleeping in the building, but in different places. People stake their claim and everyone mostly respects that."

I got up. So did Ben.

"Hey, Robyn?" Nick said.

I looked at him.

"You should dress down a little. Your boyfriend too."

CHAPTER **SEVENTEEN**

We stopped by my dad's place so that I could struggle into my oldest pair of jeans and my rattiest sweatshirt. I found a paint-splattered T-shirt and an old jacket that belonged to my father for Ben. Then we drove to Beej's place. She was waiting on the front steps of a narrow two-story house on a rundown street. She glanced at Ben's car but didn't come toward it until I called to her. She threw her backpack onto the seat beside her and thrust a gloved hand at Ben. "Hi, I'm Beej," she said.

"Ben," Ben said, shaking her hand.

"Nice car," Beej said.

"Thanks."

That's when she noticed that my jacket was buttoned over a cast and sling.

"What happened to you?" she said.

"I broke my arm."

She didn't ask how. She just buckled up and gave Ben directions.

"Take a left," Beej said twenty minutes later.

Ben pulled up to the curb a few blocks later.

I gazed around but didn't see anything resembling an abandoned warehouse. "This can't be the place," I said. All I saw were office towers, nice restaurants, and a massive hotel, probably the one where Nick had gone to clean up.

"You think anyone will talk to us if you drive up like Cinderella in this carriage?" Beej said. "We park here and we walk. You brought a flashlight, right?"

"Flashlight?"

Beej rolled her eyes. "I didn't think so."

"What do we need flashlights for?" I asked.

"It's an abandoned warehouse," Beej said. "You think they keep the lights on?" She rummaged in her backpack, produced two flashlights, and handed one to me.

"I'm not sure I like the sound of this," Ben said. "Maybe I should go and you girls should stay in the car."

"If you want my opinion, *you* girls should stay in the car," Beej said. "I can take care of this myself."

Ben bristled.

"It'll be fine, Ben," I said. "They're just people, right?"

"Right," Beej said sourly. "We're just people."

"I didn't mean—"

"You guys are strangers," Beej said, "even if you are wearing your best ripped jeans. I don't care how many cups of coffee you served at some shelter. You're still going to make people nervous. If one of you wants to come with me, okay. But both? No way."

"I'll go," I said.

"But, Robyn—"

Beej had already let herself out.

"I'll be fine," I told Ben. I scrambled to catch up with Beej.

"That guy's rich, right?" Beej said as we walked briskly away from the car.

"His family's well off," I admitted.

She shook her head. "That figures."

As we walked, the scenery quickly changed from the office towers and restaurants to old brick warehouses and factories. In some buildings, all the windows were broken. Others were in the process of being torn down.

"That's the place," Beej said, pointing to an enormous brick building. A couple of scruffy-looking men huddled at one corner of it, passing a bottle back and forth. "We might as well start with those guys."

She marched over to the two men. Neither of them was wearing gloves or boots, despite the cold. One was dressed in several layers of clothing, while the other had on a thin ski jacket and a pair of grimy khakis.

"Hey," Beej said.

The two men looked first at her, then at me.

"You guys know Nick?" Beej said.

They shrugged and shook their heads.

"This tall," Beej said, holding her hand up. "Black hair, scar here." She drew a line across her cheek.

"Show them the picture," I said.

Beej looked sharply at me, then dug in her backpack, pulled out a photograph, and showed it to the two men. One shook his head. The other looked down at the ground. Beej nudged me. I followed her.

"I could do better by myself," she said. Suddenly she raised a hand and waved. "Hey! Hey, Edmond."

A young guy in the distance wearing an overcoat turned at the sound of her voice. He nodded at her and stared sullenly at me. Beej hurried toward him.

"Edmond. How ya doin'?" she said.

Edmond mumbled an answer. His eyes were still on me. Beej moved between us, blocking his view.

"Edmond, do you remember my friend Nick?" Beej said. "I think you met him one time."

Edmond mumbled again.

"Are you staying here, Edmond?" Beej said. "Nick's been staying here."

Edmond peered around Beej at me.

"Someone went into Nick's stuff," Beej said. "I'm trying to find out who it was."

Edmond said something else before shuffling away.

"Why don't you go back to the car with your boyfriend?" Beej said. "Nobody here is going to talk to you. I know you're trying to help Nick, but—" She spotted a girl with purple hair and a young guy with a dog. "Hey, I know them. They were in one of my videos. Head to the car. I'll meet you there." She jogged off to catch up with the girl, the guy, and the dog.

I glanced around, trying to orient myself using Nick's sketch, and decided to take a look inside the building.

It was dark inside. The windows were set high in the walls and so caked with grime light only came in through the broken panes. I shone my flashlight around. The place was deserted, but heaps of garbage and a few mangy sleeping bags told me that it hadn't always been.

Nick had said that he'd been sleeping in the basement. I looked around for a way down. There was a big metal door on the far side of the room, open to a concrete stairwell. I aimed my light toward the bottom and stood for a moment, listening, before starting down the stairs.

It got blacker and blacker with every step I took. I hesitated. But Nick had chosen to live there rather than to stay with his aunt or move back into my dad's building. That was enough to spur me on. I wanted to figure out what had happened to Mr. Schuster's coins. But I also wanted to understand what had happened to Nick.

There was another door at the bottom of the stairs. I eased it open and saw a long corridor studded with a dozen more doors. I shone the light around, located an old push broom nearby, and I propped the door behind me open with it. Then I followed my flashlight beam toward the place marked with an *X* on Nick's sketch. One of the doors off the corridor was open. It led to a small room that was empty except for a few layers of old newspaper on the floor and a rolled-up sleeping bag.

Nick was right. It was warmer down in the basement than it was upstairs, out of the wind and with no broken windows to let in the cold. But my breath still plumed in front of me.

Finally, I pushed open the door to the room that Nick had marked as his on the sketch. The floor was clean, as if it had been swept. A couple of wooden crates stood against one wall. A huge pile of cinder blocks filled one corner of the room, just as Nick had described. He'd told me he stashed his backpack in the pile each time he went to the hotel. I set my flashlight down and struggled to move a few of the blocks using my good arm. I peered into the hollowed-out interior, but there was nothing to see. I still couldn't believe that Nick had slept there instead of asking for help. I thought about Nick lying on the cold floor with nothing below him but a cheap sleeping bag. What a way to have to live. I swept my light around one more time and then stepped back out into the corridor.

Someone grabbed me from behind—an all-too-familiar feeling—and I screamed. My flashlight clattered to the floor. I was plunged into darkness.

CHAPTER **EIGHTEEN**

Whoever grabbed me had seized me by my broken arm. Pain seared from my wrist to my elbow as I struggled to break free.

I heard footsteps and saw a circle of light jagging toward me. There was a loud oomph as someone else made contact with the person who had grabbed me. My attacker slammed into the wall behind me and slid to the ground.

"Robyn, are you okay?" It was Ben.

He shone the light at the figure sitting dazed on the concrete floor. I collapsed against Ben. He wrapped his arms around me and held me tightly.

"I was watching you two from across the street," he said. "When I saw you go into the building alone, I got worried."

I was shaking all over. When those hands had closed around me, I'd thought the same man who dragged me down the alley had followed me into the basement. But looking down at the grizzled old man slumped there, legs splayed out in front of him, I wasn't so sure. He was wearing an overcoat and battered construction boots. A hat with earflaps sat atop his long, thin face. His hands, which he held in front of his face to shield his eyes from the flashlight glare, were red and gnarled. He didn't look strong enough to drag anyone down an alley—especially someone who was kicking and struggling like I had been.

I heard more footsteps and another voice.

"Nice going." Ben swung around. His beam landed on Beej's face. "You just decked Earl."

"Earl?"

Beej brushed past us and knelt down in front of the old man.

"Hey, Earl. It's Beej." She shone her own flashlight on her face. "Are you okay?"

Earl nodded, but he still looked stunned.

"Are you staying here, Earl?" Beej said.

Earl nodded again.

"Come on." Beej grabbed him by one elbow and tugged. Earl didn't budge. Beej looked around. "Anyone care to help out here?"

Ben released me and grabbed Earl's other elbow. Together they tugged him to his feet.

"Earl's harmless," Beej said. "Wish I could say the same for you two." She turned to the old man again. "Hey, Earl, you know Nick?" Beej described him. Earl nodded and muttered something back. "Yeah, he's a good guy," Beej agreed. "But he's in trouble. I'm trying to find out if you saw anyone down here, maybe trying to get into Nick's stuff?"

Earl looked pointedly at me.

"Besides her," Beej said.

"Show him the pic—"

Beej took out the photograph and shone the light on it.

"Have you seen this person around here?" she said.

Earl stared at the photograph for what seemed an eternity. I wondered if he was even clued in to what Beej was saying. Finally, he shook his head.

"Are you sure?" I said.

Beej gave me a sharp look. "He gave you an answer."

"But is he sure?" I turned to Earl. "Are you sure, Earl?"

Earl stayed focused on Beej and shook his head again.

"Okay. Thanks, Earl," Beej said.

She aimed her flashlight at Ben. "Give him some cash," she said. "It's the least you can do."

Ben handed me his flashlight. He dug his wallet out, grabbed a couple of bills, and held them out to Earl. Earl just looked at them. Beej snatched them from Ben and pressed them into Earl's hands. Then Earl leaned toward Beej and whispered something in her ear. She looked at me and followed him down the corridor. At first I couldn't hear what they were saying. Then I heard Beej say, "Do you remember when?" Earl mumbled something more that I couldn't hear. "And definitely that day?" Beej said.

I shone Ben's light on them in time to see Earl nod. Then he shuffled off into the darkness.

"You take care, Earl, okay?" Beej called after him. She bent down and picked up the flashlight I had dropped. It wouldn't work. "You're paying me back for this," she said.

"I thought he was attacking her," Ben said as we headed back to the car.

"He thought she was breaking into his place," Beej said. "And he can't call the cops like you can. He has to take care of it himself."

Ben unlocked the car and we got in.

"What did he say?" I asked Beej.

"He saw someone around the place the day before Mr. Schuster's coins were stolen."

"Who?"

"He doesn't know. He'd never seen the person before."

"Person?" I said. That didn't sound good. "A man or a woman?"

"He's not sure. He just said he saw someone around the building—someone who didn't belong."

"Did he actually see this person in Nick's room?"

"Well, no."

"Did he describe the person?" Ben said.

"He just said that he—"

"—or she," I muttered.

"—was wearing a warm jacket with the hood up. He couldn't see the face."

"I don't suppose he remembers the jacket color?" I asked.

"Black."

I groaned. "Did he say anything else about it?" There must be thousands of black jackets in the city. "For all we know, it could have been some other homeless person."

"That's not what he said." Beej was losing her patience. "He said it was someone who didn't belong."

"What does that even mean?"

"He can tell the difference. *I* can tell the difference."

"Sorry," I muttered. "Anyway, he said he saw this person the day before the coins were stolen, not the day of the theft—as far as he can remember."

Beej glared at me. "He's homeless, not stupid. If he said it was the day before, it was the day before. He'd just come back from having the hot lunch at St. Stephen's."

"Several downtown churches serve hot lunches," Ben interjected. "Each one operates on a different day."

"That's right," Beej said, regarding him with new interest. "He says he saw the person on the day he ate at St. Stephen's. It's his favorite place for lunch."

"So all we have to do is tell the police—" Ben began.

"Tell them what?" Beej and I said in unison.

"I thought the whole point was to see if someone planted stolen property on Nick while he was out," Ben said. "Doesn't this help?"

"Yeah, but our star witness is Earl," I said. "And he can't describe the person except to say he was wearing a black jacket."

"Still, it's something," Ben said. "Just because he's homeless doesn't mean the cops won't listen."

Beej rolled her eyes. "It's not just that he's homeless. He knows me. He's in one of my videos. And I know Nick. When the cops picked him up, he was at my place. Given that, do you really think they'll believe anything Earl tells them?"

"Assuming they listen to him at all," I added. He hadn't even seen him or her on the day of the robbery. It was the day before. Without more to go on, I couldn't see how that proved a thing.

We were on our way back to Henri's when I had an idea.

"Did you take any other pictures?" I asked Beej.

"I took a bunch. But you said you wanted—"

"Did you take any outside?"

"Sure. Why?" Her eyes lit up. "My camera's back at the house."

Ben changed direction and drove Beej back to her place so she could pick up her camera. She scrolled through the pictures until she found the one she was looking for. Two of the four people in it were wearing black jackets. We drove back to the warehouse. Ben and I stayed in the car while Beej went in to search for Earl. When she returned, she was smiling.

"He may not be able to describe the person," she said, "but he's positive about the jacket." She held the camera out to me and tapped the screen.

I stared at the display. "He's sure?" I said.

This time she didn't snap at me. She just smiled and said, "Trust me, Robyn. Earl doesn't forget a warm jacket."

. . .

We went back to Henri's place. While Henri made tea, Beej wandered around the house, staring at all the paintings. Her jaw dropped when I told her that Henri was the artist.

"Beej is a photographer and videographer," I told Henri. "You should see her stuff."

Henri asked her about her work. Beej answered shyly. And when Henri invited her upstairs to see her studio, Beej's face lit up. While she was gone, Nick and Ben and I sat at Henri's dining room table. I filled Nick in on what we had found out.

"Are you sure?" Nick said. "Does that even make sense?"

"They all knew where you were staying," I said. "Elliot had you checked out, remember? He hired a private investigator. He must have followed you to the warehouse."

"But Earl saw him the day before the robbery," Nick said. "How does that help?"

"It proves that someone not only knew where you lived but was actually there—maybe the day before the robbery and the day of. When you came back from the hotel that afternoon, you didn't see a crowbar anywhere, did you?"

Ben gave me a baffled look.

Nick shook his head. "But I didn't look for one, either," he said. "I dug out my bag and headed out to meet Beej. She insisted I come to her place when she found out where I was staying. So I took my stuff over there. Then I—." He hesitated and looked at Ben. He'd been going to say that then he went to my dad's place and climbed onto the roof. "Anyway, I slept at Beej's that night. On the couch. The cops showed up the next day and arrested me."

Beej came back downstairs.

"Have you seen Henri's studio?" She was clearly impressed. "She said I was welcome to come over anytime. She probably doesn't mean it, right?"

"Of course she means it. Henri loves people who love art," I said.

Beej sank down onto a chair to digest this.

"I still don't get it," Nick said. "If Earl's right, why did that guy at the mall try to scare me into handing over the coins? Why did he attack you for the same reason?"

Ben looked at me. "You never said anything about that guy wanting stolen coins."

"I didn't want to worry you," I said, even though that wasn't the real reason.

"You think he was trying to make sure I looked guilty?" Nick said.

The thought had occurred to me. Now I wasn't so sure.

"I think someone's looking for those coins and really believes you know where they are," I said. "I think that's why Beej's place was broken into."

"What?" I hadn't told Nick about that. I guess Beej hadn't, either. He looked at her, concerned.

"Someone trashed my place," she said. "No big deal. It's not like we had a lot of expensive stuff or anything."

When Nick frowned, I explained. "You were found with just a few coins on you—the least valuable ones. The rest of the coins weren't recovered. Someone must have thought that you stashed them. When they didn't find the coins, they threatened you."

"So now what?" Beej said.

"We should call the police," Ben said.

"We don't have anything credible to tell them," I explained gently, "except that Earl, who knows Beej, who's a friend of Nick's, says he recognizes a jacket that he saw near the building before the theft even happened. But there must be something we can do."

"Like what?" Beej said.

We all looked at one another. No one said a word.

.   .   .

Eventually Beej had to go. "But you know where to find me if you need me, right, Nick?"

Nick nodded.

Ben glanced at his watch. "I have to go too. I'm supposed to babysit my sister. Are you coming, Robyn?"

I shook my head. "I promised my dad that I would stay here."

Ben looked across the table at Nick. I could tell he didn't want to leave me, but what could he do? I walked him to the door.

. . .

Henri, Nick, and I had an early, awkward dinner. Henri was talkative, as usual. Nick was polite, but he directed all of his comments at Henri and didn't look at me once. After eating, he offered to clean up. When he finished, he retreated to his room. Henri gave me a look but didn't say anything. I stayed at the table and thought about what Earl had seen and what Isobel had told me. I thought about Mr. Schuster too and wondered what would happen if Elliot couldn't find Orion a good home. What would Mr. Schuster do then? Would he really refuse to go to a home?

I wondered if anyone had taken Orion for a walk that day but couldn't imagine that Elliot had managed to find a dog walker so quickly. Orion was probably cooped up in the basement again. Poor, poor Orion . . .

That gave me an idea.

It was only seven o' clock. If I hurried, I could make it. I called to Henri that I was going out for a while. Nick came out of his room and watched me pull on my coat.

"Going to hang with the boyfriend after all, huh?" he said.

"No. I'm—"

"It's okay," he said. "You don't owe me any explanation."

"I'll be back as soon as I can," I said. "You'll still be here, right? Because I need you to be here, Nick. It's important."

He nodded curtly.

"I'd take you with me now if I could," I said.

"Whatever."

"Please be here when I get back, Nick."

"I said I would be. What's the matter? Don't you trust me?"

CHAPTER **NINETEEN**

Nick was in Henri's living room flipping through a magazine when I got back an hour later. He didn't look up as I came through the door.

"I'm going to need your help a little later," I said.

He stopped flipping pages.

"I wouldn't ask," I said, "but this is something I can't do by myself."

"Why don't you ask what's-his-name?" he said.

"Because it's something only you can do." I could tell he wanted to ask what it was, but his pride wouldn't let him. "It's been a long day, and my arm hurts. I'm going to take a nap. I'll knock on your door when I'm ready. Okay?"

He didn't say yes. But he didn't say no, either.

. . .

Nick was fully dressed when he answered my knock later that night. He didn't ask why I wanted his help. He didn't even say a word until we got back, and then the only thing he said was, "Are you sure Henri won't mind?"

"Pretty sure," I said. "Nothing ever throws her. 'Night, Nick."

"Robyn?"

I turned to face him. He looked at me for what seemed like an eternity.

"What's wrong with me?" he said.

"What do you mean?"

"Is it because I'm broke all the time? Is that why you didn't wait for me? Or would you have gone for him anyway, even if I hadn't left?"

"I didn't know where you were, Nick. You just took off. You told Beej you were going. You even told Mr. Schuster. Why didn't you tell me?"

"Didn't tell you?" He looked baffled. "What are you talking about? It was all in the letter."

"Letter? What letter?"

"The one I wrote you. The longest thing I ever wrote."

"Why didn't you just call me?"

"I thought you'd get mad—I knew you would. You would've told me not to go. But I had to."

"So you wrote a letter?"

"Yeah."

"I never got it."

He stared at me. "But I took it to your house myself. I wanted to make sure you got it as soon as you got back from your trip."

"I never got any letter, Nick. My mom would have told me."

"I went to your house. I was putting it in the mailbox when this man came out."

"Man? You mean Ted?"

"He didn't say who he was. He looked like a handyman. He said he was doing some work for your mom."

"Zeke." Zeke had been doing odd jobs for my mother since before she and my father separated. She'd hired him to install built-in bookshelves and cupboards in the basement as part of her continual quest to have a place for everything and keep everything in its place. "Big man, gray hair, paint-splattered overalls?"

"That's him," Nick said. "He said he'd put the letter inside where it'd be safe."

"What did it say?"

"That I had to go out west for a while and that I wasn't sure how long I'd be gone. I left a number where you could call me when you got back—you know, after you got over being mad. But you never called."

"Why didn't you call me?"

He looked down at the floor.

"No more lies, Nick, remember?"

"I would've. But I got locked up."

"Locked up? What for? What did you do?"

His eyes flashed as they met mine again. "See? That's what I wanted to avoid—you talking to me that way, assuming I must have done something wrong."

I tried to calm down, but it was hard because he was telling the story in bits and pieces instead of just laying it all out.

"Why were you locked up, Nick?"

"It doesn't matter anymore. Not when I'm probably going to end up there again."

He started to close the door. I pushed it open and stepped inside.

"It matters to me," I said. "Tell me."

"Joey called me," Nick said.

Joey. Nick's stepbrother. It figured.

"See? There you go," Nick said. "You always get that same look on your face when I mention Joey. I know you don't like him, Robyn. But he's my brother." Joey was in prison, but that didn't matter to Nick. Nick would do anything for Joey, no matter what kind of trouble it might land him in. "That's why I didn't want to tell you where I was going. I wanted to see how things worked out first."

"Okay, I'm sorry," I said. "What did he want?"

"He said he needed my help."

I had to struggle to keep that same look off my face. The last time Joey had asked Nick for help, Nick had almost ended up in jail himself.

"He said that the last couple of times he talked to Angie, he got the idea something was wrong, but she wouldn't tell him what."

Angie is Joey's girlfriend. She'd been pregnant when Joey went to prison. She lived out west with their baby son.

"Joey asked me to go out and check on her. To make sure she was okay. I didn't know how long I'd be gone. I mean, if something was wrong, if Angie needed help . . ."

"Is she okay?"

"She is now. She finally found a place she could afford. But when I got there, she was living with her sister and this creep brother-in-law who was always giving her a hard time. Always drunk and calling Joey a loser and telling Jack terrible things about him. She didn't want Jack growing up like that. The guy told her to move out if she didn't like it. She wanted to. She was looking. But it takes time, you know? And it's hard with a little baby."

His hands clenched as he told the story.

"Anyway, I went out there and the sister let me sleep on the couch. But her husband started in right away, giving me a hard time too. I kept my cool—well, much as I could. But I talked back to him one time when Angie and her sister were out and it was just me and Jack and him at the house. He took a swing at me—and ended up with a black eye. I got arrested. He accused me of stuff I didn't do, Robyn. Then I got jammed up because I have a record. They said I could only be released to an adult relative, but I didn't have any out there."

"What about your aunt? Couldn't she have done something?"

"I didn't tell them about her. She would just have got mad at me. She didn't even know I was gone. I told them the truth, Robyn. I said I lived on my own. Anyway, there was no one to release me to, and they needed to be sure that I'd show up for my court date. So they detained me. They said I could call my family or my lawyer. Anyone else had to be on an approved list, and you weren't. Angie offered to call you for me, but I was afraid you wouldn't understand."

"Haven't I always believed in you, Nick?"

He bowed his head for a moment.

"Angie told me that you never called. I was afraid maybe you'd already given up on me. Anyway, Angie finally got her brother-in-law to withdraw the charges. I called you as soon as I got out"—the garbled phone message—"and when you didn't call back . . ." He shrugged. "Anyway, that's all in the past now, huh?"

"What about the girl who gave you that money?" I said.

Nick shook his head in disbelief. "That was weird. I was hitching home, and this guy let me off at a gas station along the highway. I had maybe five dollars in my pocket. And I found this purse. Just sitting there. I looked inside and found a name and a number, so I called. It turned out the purse belonged to this girl who had stopped there only about an hour earlier. She didn't even realize her purse was missing until I called her. She drove back to the gas station."

I waited for him to explain the thousand dollars in cash.

"Turns out she's a model. You should have seen her. She looked like she belonged in a magazine. She was that pretty." His cheeks turned pink. "Not as pretty as you, though."

"Right."

"Anyway, she was on her way back to town after visiting her mother. She had to catch a plane. She was on her way to Paris for a shoot. And, I don't know, we got to talking. We had a lot in common."

"Oh?"

"Yeah. She had this terrible stepdad. She hated the guy. He'd hit her mom." Nick's stepfather had beaten his mother—so badly that the last time he did it, she died of her injuries. "Her mom finally left the guy. Sarah said now that she was making all this money, she was going to buy her mom nice things. Then she offered me a lift. When she found out I didn't know where I was going and that I wasn't sure I could get my old job back, she gave me a thousand dollars. Just like that, like it was nothing. She said I could pay her back when I got rich and famous. Crazy, huh?"

Nick was smiling when he finished the story, but then he grew serious again. "Would it have made a difference if you had got my letter?"

If I'd read Nick's letter, I would never have agreed to go out with Ben. But it hadn't worked out that way. And Ben had been so good to me. He'd even been willing to help me help Nick. I couldn't pretend that he didn't exist. I had to consider his feelings—didn't I?

"Probably," I said. "But—"

"But?"

"What I'm trying to say is—"

"It's okay. It doesn't matter anymore," Nick said. "You have a real boyfriend now, someone who can give you things I never could."

Ben was all that, for sure. But in my heart I wondered, Could he give me what I really wanted?

.   .   .

I got up early—well, earlier than Henri. Nick was already awake and was outside in Henri's tiny backyard. He came in for a moment when he saw me.

"Are you sure you're going to be okay?" he said.

"I'm just going to find out what's going on," I said. "I've got my phone. If anything happens, I'll call 9-1-1."

"I wish I could go with you," he said.

"I'll be fine."

I grabbed one of Henri's oatmeal-raisin muffins to eat on the way and left the house.

CHAPTER TWENTY

Elliot answered the door. He was holding a piece of paper in one hand. His eyes kept skipping to it as he asked me what I was doing there.

"I know you think I lied to you," I said. "And I know you don't want me around. But I am a friend of your father's—that part's true—and someone has to walk Orion. You can come with me if you don't trust me. Or Isobel can. But it's not fair to keep Orion locked up in the basement because of something you think I did."

"The dog isn't here," Elliot said.

"What do you mean? You didn't send him to a shelter, did you?"

Isobel appeared at the door behind her father. "Someone kidnapped Orion," she said.

"What? When?"

"Elliot, close the door," said Claudia in a loud, shrill voice. "It's freezing in here."

To my surprise, Elliot didn't slam the door in my face. Instead, he stood aside to let me into the front hall. Claudia was framed in the doorway to the kitchen. Connor was on the stairs, looking down at me.

"It was that friend of yours, wasn't it?" Claudia said. "He took the dog."

"Nick?" I said. "Why would he do that?"

"Out of spite," Claudia said. "Because Elliot fired him. Because Elliot told the police where to find him."

I turned back to Elliot. "When did it happen?"

"Last night."

"You didn't hear anything?"

"Nothing out of the ordinary," Elliot said. "That dog barks so much I don't pay attention anymore."

"Have you called the police?"

Elliot held the sheet of paper in front of me. It was a ransom note.

"It says no police," he said. "The kidnapper wants the coins. If he doesn't get them, he'll kill the dog. If I call the police, he'll kill the dog. Do you have any idea what it would do to my father if someone hurt that dog? And you can bet that I'd be held responsible."

"Why would Nick kidnap Orion and demand the coins as ransom?" I said slowly. "Are you saying that you don't think that Nick stole the coins?"

"He stole them all right," Connor said. "He was caught with them in his backpack."

"Why would anyone think we know where the coins are?" Elliot said. "They were stolen from us."

"From Grandpa," Isobel said quietly.

"You should call the police," I said.

"Robyn's right," Isobel said.

Elliot wheeled around to her. "Are you insane?" he said. "Do you have any idea what the police would think if they saw this note?"

Isobel's voice trembled a little when she said, "They'd think that someone took Orion."

"They'd think that someone in this house knows where those coins are," Elliot said angrily. That's exactly what had gone through my mind after I was attacked—if I said anything to the police, they would think that Nick knew where the coins were. "They'd think that someone must have done something that made these people think they could blackmail us by taking the dog and demanding the coins as ransom." He waved the note in her face. She jumped back, startled. "And what do you think would happen when the police reported that to the insurance company? They'd think that I took the coins and filed a false claim. They'd think I was trying to defraud them. We'd never get the money."

"You mean, Grandpa would never get the money," Isobel said.

Elliot wheeled back around to me. "Maybe some other lowlife heard about the theft and decided to take advantage of the situation. Maybe they found out how much your boyfriend cares about the dog, but they don't know how to contact him, so they left this note here.

Why don't you tell him what happened? Tell him if he doesn't hand over the coins, the dog will die."

"Daddy!" Isobel looked shocked.

"I need that dog back," Elliot said desperately. He let out a long shuddery sigh. "My father already thinks I hate the animal. He thinks I want to get rid of it. He's been mad at me for years. Sometimes I think he's been mad at me my whole life. I came here to help him out, and the first thing that happens is that his coin collection gets stolen. And then, because I tried to protect it by getting it insured, the insurance company gets suspicious. Now his dog has vanished while it was in my care."

He seemed genuinely upset. That was enough to convince me that I was finally on the right track.

"At first I thought you were the one who got someone to threaten me," I said.

"Threaten you?" Elliot said, stunned. "What are you talking about?"

"Someone hurt Robyn," Isobel said.

I told Elliot what had happened.

"The man wanted me to tell Nick to hand over the coins. He said if he didn't, someone would get hurt. He shoved me around to show he was serious. My arm got broken."

"Good Lord," Elliot said. "And you thought I was responsible for that?"

"Well, if I'd reported the attack, the police would have told the insurance company, and they would have believed the coins had been stolen. And that Nick did it."

"My dad would never do anything like that," Isobel said.

"I was attacked two blocks from here, right after I left this house on Friday," I said, focusing on Elliot. "Whoever attacked me knew exactly where to find me. How could he have known that? He wanted me to give a message to Nick. How did he even know that I knew Nick?"

Elliot stared mutely at me.

"But you *did* know," I said. "Connor found out. And Isobel knew that I used to go out with Nick. So someone in this house must have attacked me or arranged for me to be attacked. I thought it could only be you."

"Why me?" Elliot said.

"Because I thought you staged the robbery and hid the coins."

"That's ridiculous—he's my father!"

"First," I said, "because you were the one who pushed your father to insure his coins as soon as you found out how valuable they were."

"That was my wife's idea, not mine," Elliot said in a small, strangled voice.

"Second, if the insurance company had paid the claim, you could have given the money to your father and then sold the coins that you had stashed. Third, you need the money. Your business is in trouble." Elliot turned red in the face. He was probably wondering how I knew that, but he didn't say I was wrong. "You don't even let your wife have a credit card. Fourth, you've asked your father for money before, but he's always turned you down. You even sent your wife to ask on your behalf, but he turned her down too."

"I did no such thing."

"She was here last fall," I said. "If you don't believe me, ask her."

Elliot turned to Claudia with what looked like a mixture of fury and disbelief. "Is this true? Did you come here and ask Dad for money?"

"Elliot, it's not what you think," Claudia said meekly.

He shook his head in disgust.

"Fifth," I continued, "your wife knew about Nick's past and should have told you. But you acted as if she hadn't."

Elliot's eyes focused hard on his wife.

"You knew about this boy too?" he said.

Claudia didn't answer.

"Sixth, you had Nick checked out. You knew where he was staying. And the day the coins were stolen, you left for a meeting but then told your family that the meeting was really for the following week—which means that you have no alibi for that afternoon."

"That afternoon?" I could tell Elliot was baffled. "But the coins weren't stolen until that night. We were all—"

I didn't let him finish. "And, finally, you've been making it sound as if your father can't manage his own affairs. If you could get yourself made his guardian, you would control his finances. You could bail out your business."

"I would never...," Elliot said. "I love my father. I want things to be right between us." He turned to his wife. "Why didn't you tell me you came here to ask him for money?"

She said nothing. I guess I couldn't blame her.

"Then I found out that your wife was the last person to see the coins before they were stolen," I said. I turned to face Claudia. "All of you said you were out of the house that afternoon. When you came back home before dinner, you went upstairs to change. You and your husband are using the back bedroom where Mr. Schuster kept his coin collection. You told the police that you were the only one who went into that room before leaving for dinner and that the coins were there before you left." I'd seen that in the police report that I'd found in Mr. Schuster's den. "You said you saw them when you were changing, but when Connor and Isobel went up there after you got back from the restaurant, they were gone."

"That's right," Claudia said.

"Is it?" I said.

"What are you talking about?" Elliot said. "You doubt my wife?"

I turned back to him. "You were supposed to meet your family at the restaurant, weren't you?"

"Yes, but I don't see—"

"But when you realized you'd mixed up the meeting date, you came back to the house. I bet your wife was surprised."

Elliot glanced at her.

"Did you go upstairs at all?"

"I wanted to take a quick shower," Elliot said. "But Claudia said there was no time."

"She didn't want you to go upstairs," I said. "I think she was afraid that if you did, you'd have seen that the coins were already gone."

"That's ridiculous!" Claudia said.

Elliot stared at her.

"Nick didn't take those coins," I said. "I know that for a fact. That means someone must have planted a few coins in his backpack and left that crowbar in the building where he was staying. But the only time Nick was away from his backpack was for a short time that afternoon— the same as every afternoon. So whoever planted those coins on Nick must have done it that afternoon, not that evening. Where were you that afternoon, Mrs. Schuster?"

"I was at the hospital with Isobel."

I glanced at Isobel. An expression of horror was creeping onto her face.

"Not . . . the whole time, Mom," Isobel said in a small voice. "You left me at the hospital at noon. You didn't come back until a little after three, remember? You said you were going to replace the glass you broke that morning."

"What glass?" Elliot said.

"I dropped one of your father's glasses. I wanted to replace it."

"You told Isobel that you went to every department store in town, but you couldn't find one that matched," I said.

"That's right," Claudia said.

"You didn't buy anything at those stores, did you?" I said.

"As I said, I couldn't find what I was looking for."

"But since you didn't find a matching glass, there's no record to show that you were actually in any of those stores."

"Are you calling me a liar?" Claudia said, bristling.

"When you were here in the fall, Orion was still sleeping in the basement. But by the time you came back with the rest of the family, Mr. Schuster had moved him to the back bedroom, where he kept the coins. But you had no way of knowing that. One of the first things you did when you came here that first night was to go up to the room. You didn't even hesitate when you heard him barking."

"Elliot's father said he was well-behaved. He said I shouldn't be afraid of him."

"You wanted to check on the coins. Were you making sure they were still there? But you startled Orion and he reacted. So you saw to it that he was locked in the basement."

"My mom was scared, that's all," Isobel said. "She didn't want to hurt Orion. Right, Mom?"

I could imagine how Isobel was feeling. If someone had been saying the kinds of things about my mother that I was saying about hers, I'd have reacted the same way. But I wanted to clear this up—and clear Nick—once and for all.

"Having Orion in the basement was a big help to you," I said to Claudia. "If he'd stayed in that room, it would have been a lot harder for you to get to the coins. As soon as you heard that Mr. Schuster was sick, you offered to come here by yourself to look after him." Isobel had told me that. "That would have made things even easier. You could have staged a robbery much more easily, without so many people around. When your husband insisted on coming with you, you had to get creative."

She looked at Elliot. "This is crazy," she said.

"You knew where Nick was staying," I continued. "You have no alibi for that afternoon. As for what happened to me, you got a phone call just before I left here on Friday. Did you tell someone that I was leaving the house?"

Elliot shook his head slowly. "Claudia, what's going on?"

"Elliot, you have to believe me. I have no idea where those coins are."

"Who is Mr. Jones?" I said. "Is he the one who attacked me?"

"Claudia?" Elliot said, his tone a warning.

"Oh, Elliot." Claudia's voice was full of anguish.

Elliot's shoulders slumped. "Tell me you haven't been gambling again."

Isobel was as confused as I was. "What are you talking about, Dad?"

"Mom has a gambling problem," Connor said with a distinct lack of sympathy. "Why do you think Dad took

217

away her credit card? Why do you think he made us all come here? He was afraid if he left her alone, she'd gamble the house away."

"Claudia, please tell me you had nothing to do with what happened to Robyn or to those coins," Elliot said.

Claudia started to sob. "Elliot, I'm so sorry."

"Oh my God," Elliot said.

Isobel stared at her mother. I thought she was going to start crying too.

"He said if I didn't pay what I owed, someone would get hurt. He knew all about the kids—their names, where they go to school, everything. I didn't know what else to do."

"Tell me where those coins are this instant," Elliot said. "I am not going to disappoint my father again. It was bad enough when I had to miss my mother's funeral to drag you out of that casino. When I almost lost everything trying to cover your debts. You promised me."

Claudia wept quietly. "I don't have the coins, Elliot. I swear I don't. Robyn's right. I took them. I took them that afternoon and I hid them. But they were insured. It wasn't like your father was going to lose everything. He would have been compensated."

Connor snorted in derision. "Grandpa doesn't have those coins for what they're worth," he said. "He has them because he loves them. Some of them are impossible to replace. You can't just go to a store and buy more."

"Where are they, Claudia?" Elliot said.

"That boy has them. Nick. That's what the police said. He broke into the house and stole them. The police arrested him, Elliot."

"Mom, I don't understand," Isobel said.

"Neither do I," Elliot said coldly.

"I hid the coins," Claudia said again. "I took the screen off the kitchen window—it was falling off anyway—and left the window open a little so the police would think the thief came in that way." That explained what my dad had told me. I guessed that she didn't know the window didn't open wide enough to let anyone slip through. "Then you said that the side door had been forced open. But I didn't do that. I didn't touch the door. So when you told us to search the house for anything else missing, I checked to make sure the coins were where I'd hidden them.

"But they were gone," Claudia continued. "You said Nick must have broken into the house and taken them. One of the neighbors said they had seen him lurking around earlier that day. That's what must have happened! Because I don't know where they are!"

"Is that what you told Mr. Jones?" I said. "It would explain why the place where Nick was staying was broken into. Someone was looking for the coins. And that day at the mall, someone pushed Nick to scare him into handing them over. That's how your father fell down the escalator— because Nick was shoved into him. I think the man who pushed Nick had been watching his aunt's house. Then, when Nick didn't hand over the coins, I was attacked."

"And now my father's dog has been kidnapped."

"Elliot, I'm so sorry," Claudia whimpered. "But I don't know where those coins are. I swear I don't."

And Mr. Jones had lost his patience. He wanted the money Claudia owed him, and he had done his best to get it. But where were the coins now?

At first I had been confused by what Earl said he'd seen. But after everything I had just heard, it was starting to make sense. I turned to Connor.

"You don't have an alibi for that afternoon, either, do you?" I said.

CHAPTER **TWENTY-ONE**

"Connor?" Elliot said. "You think Connor knows where the coins are?"

"I was at the library," Connor said defiantly.

"Reference library," I said. "Hundreds of people go in and out all day, and no one can take out any books, so you probably thought that nobody'd be able to check if you were really there. But they have security cameras. The police could check if someone asked them to."

Connor tried to look like he didn't care, but I saw a hint of worry in his eyes.

"I know you heard your dad say where Nick was staying. I also know you went there the day before the robbery. Someone saw you, Connor. Someone can identify you." Well, they could identify his jacket. "What were you doing?"

"Nothing."

"Connor?" his father said sternly.

"I wanted to see where he lived, okay?" Connor said angrily. "I wanted to see why Grandpa thought he was such a big deal."

"You went back again the day of the robbery and planted the crowbar and coins, didn't you?"

"Connor was going to inherit those coins," Elliot said. "What reason could he have for stealing them?"

"I don't know," I said. "But the coins the police found in Nick's backpack were the least valuable in the whole collection. You and your wife don't know much about coins. But you know, don't you, Connor? You were careful to use the coins that didn't matter to frame Nick, the ones that weren't worth much."

"This is ridiculous," Elliot said.

"Did you do it because you were jealous of Nick?" I continued. "Your grandfather had been spending a lot of time with him. He was teaching him all about coins. He was even planning to leave him part of the collection. I bet you weren't happy when you heard that, were you, Connor?"

"The guy's a loser," Connor said. "He did time. Isn't that what you said, Dad?"

Elliot frowned. "Connor, you didn't actually—"

"Someone had to protect Grandpa's collection," Connor said.

"Protect it from who?" Elliot said.

"From Mom. I saw the look on her face when she realized how much the coins were worth. She started nagging you about whether they were insured. Don't look at me like that, Dad. She just admitted what she did."

"We're not talking about your mother now, Connor," Elliot said.

"I heard her talking to that guy, Jones, about how much she owed him. She told him about Grandpa's collection." He looked contemptuously at his mother. "That's all you care about, isn't it? To you, the coins are just a way to pay off your debt. You don't understand—neither of you do. They're not just money, they're history. That's what Grandpa always said. They're pocket-sized pieces of history. But the only thing the two of you cared about was how much they were worth."

"Did you take those coins, Connor?"

"You're not listening," Connor said. "Mom took them. But I knew she was up to something. I pretended I was going to the library and waited until she left the house with Isobel. Then I snuck back inside. I saw her, Dad. I saw her take them, where she hid them. When she left again, I took them and put them someplace safe."

There was something I didn't understand: "Why pry open the side door? Your mom already fixed it so that it'd look like the thief came in through the kitchen window."

Connor looked at me as if I were an idiot. "If I just moved them, she might figure out that it was me. But if it looked like someone really had broken in, she'd blame someone else."

I turned to Claudia again. "And that's what you told Mr. Jones, right? That's why Beej's house was broken into. That's why Nick and I were attacked. You really thought Nick had those coins, and you needed them."

"You lied to me," Elliot said. "You stole from my father. And now some thug has my father's dog." He turned to Connor. "This ends here, do you understand? Give me the coins."

"What are you going to do with them?" Connor said. "Give them to her"—he looked disdainfully at his mother—"so she can give them to Mr. Jones? So you can get that stupid dog?"

"Connor!" Isobel said, snapping out of the daze she had been in. "Grandpa loves Orion."

"And as long as he's alive, those coins are his, not yours," Elliot said. "Connor, if you don't hand over those coins this minute, if anything happens to that dog, I'll call the police myself. And I'll tell your grandfather exactly what you did."

"I was helping him. I was protecting his coins."

"You lied—to him, to me, to everyone. You made an innocent person look guilty. The police can charge you for that, Connor. Is that what you want? What do you think it would do to your grandfather if he found out? You'd never inherit those coins. Never."

Connor stared defiantly at his father for a moment. Then he caved in.

"They're in the garage," he said. "Under Grandpa's workbench. I was going to give them back to Grandpa when he got better. Then everything got so complicated. I wasn't trying to hurt anyone, Dad. I was just trying to protect Grandpa's coins."

"And make sure he didn't leave any of them to Nick," I said sourly.

Elliot looked defeated. "I should probably call the police," he said. "But what will happen to the dog if I do?" He looked at his wife. "Do you think Jones will make good on his threat?"

"You don't have to worry about Orion," I said.

"How do you know?" Elliot said.

"I know where he is. He's in good hands."

"You have the dog?" Claudia said.

I reached into my pocket for the piece of paper Mr. Schuster had signed for me at the hospital the night before and handed it to Elliot.

"I didn't tell your father what I suspected," I said. "I thought you'd want to do that yourself. I just told him that I wanted to make sure Orion was being looked after. He gave me permission to remove him from the house last night."

"But how? We were here last night," Elliot said.

"She probably broke in," Connor said bitterly.

I ignored him. "Your father trusted Nick with a set of keys. And you said yourself that Orion barks so much, you hardly notice anymore." I'd been counting on that.

"Where is he now?" Elliot asked.

"Nick has him."

Elliot sighed. "I doubt I could find a better home for the dog than with that boy. He certainly seems to love that animal."

"He still has a court date coming up," I said. "Nick was also charged with assaulting your wife and with unlawful entry into the house."

"I'll withdraw the charges," Claudia said quietly.

"He never hit you, did he?" I said.

She shook her head.

"Then why on earth did you say he did?" Elliot asked.

"Because she really believed that Nick stole those coins," I said.

"The police said he did," Claudia said.

"And then he showed up and wanted to talk to Mr. Schuster. I bet you were surprised."

"I was afraid he would try to trade the coins for the dog."

"I bet you were also afraid that if Nick talked to Mr. Schuster, he might mention where he'd found the coins. And if he did, Mr. Schuster would know that they had been moved. That's why you claimed Nick assaulted you. You had him charged. Then you got a restraining order to keep him away from Mr. Schuster."

Claudia Schuster bowed her head and began to cry. Elliot did not go to her and hug her. He stood across the hall from her and stared at her as if she were a stranger.

CHAPTER TWENTY-TWO

Elliot Schuster might not have had the best relationship with his father, but he wasn't a thief and he wasn't completely unfeeling. He had seemed really concerned about how losing Orion would have affected Mr. Schuster. And as soon as he found out what had happened, he did the right thing. He called the police and explained everything. He insisted that all charges against Nick be dropped. He said that he would leave it up to his father to decide if he wanted to press charges against Claudia or Connor. He also said that he wanted to stop by my dad's place later to apologize to Nick. He asked me if I would agree to be there too. But first I had a stop to make.

I went from Mr. Schuster's house to my mother's house, took off my boots and coat, and stood inside for some time, wondering what could have happened to the letter Nick said he had left with Zeke.

Zeke had installed shelves and cupboards in the basement while I was away on a school trip. Since then, my mother had talked about uncluttering the main floor of the house by moving things down to those new shelves, but so far, she hadn't got around to it. I doubted she had even been in the basement since Zeke had done his installation.

I went downstairs. The shelves, which were built into one wall, stood empty. I approached them but found nothing. One by one, I opened the cupboards below the shelves.

And there, lying at the bottom of one empty cupboard, was an envelope with my name on it. Zeke must have brought it downstairs, intending to give it to my mom, then forgotten all about it.

I picked up the envelope. Inside was a letter hand written by Nick. It said exactly what he said it would say. I sank down to the floor.

.   .   .

Elliot Schuster was already at my father's place when I got back. Claudia and Connor were with him. All three of them took a step backward when they saw Orion, even though Nick had him on a tight leash. Not only did Elliot apologize to Nick—and to me—but he made Claudia and Connor apologize too. Then he said, "My father is going into a nursing home as soon as he's discharged from the hospital. He wants to know if you would be interested in adopting Orion—assuming, of course, that you're able to provide for him."

Nick's face lit up. "I know I'll be able to get a job," he said. "I got a good reference from the last place I worked." He must have meant La Folie. "And I'm going back to school. Tell Mr. Schuster that I'll take good care of Orion. And I'll bring him by for regular visits. Make sure you tell him that part."

"I will," Elliot promised. He reached for his coat. "I misjudged you, Nick," he added. "I'm sorry."

.   .   .

"Well, I can't say you two didn't cover your bases," my dad said after the Schusters had left. "But it could have turned out differently, Robbie. If Elliot really had stolen those coins, if he'd been desperate . . ."

"I knew Connor was involved, Dad. Earl was positive about the jacket he'd seen. And I knew Elliot had nothing to do with it when he told me about the ransom note. He wanted to get Orion back safely, and he had no idea where to find the coins."

My father arched an eyebrow at the mention of a ransom note. "There are elements of this story that you might not want to mention to your mother," he said. "In fact, you might want to consider not mentioning the whole thing. And, Robbie? Don't lie to me or the police again, okay?"

"Sorry, Dad."

Nick, who was sitting at the end of my father's couch, reached out to scratch Orion behind the ear. The massive dog's tail thumped happily on the hardwood floor.

"I can keep him," he said, his voice filled with awe. "I can't believe it. I can keep him."

"I'm sure he'd appreciate having a roof over his head," my father said. "Your apartment is still empty, Nick. It's yours if you want it."

Nick glanced at me. "I appreciate the offer, Mr. Hunter," he said. "But Beej has invited me to crash on her couch for now."

"Fair enough," my father said. "The apartment's there if you change your mind."

"I appreciate everything you did for me," Nick said. "You, too, Robyn." He started to get up. "I'd better get going."

"Nick, we need to talk," I said.

Nick dropped down onto the couch again.

"I have some phone calls to make," my dad said. He withdrew to his office and closed the door.

I looked at Nick.

"I don't know what would have happened if you hadn't got involved, Robyn," he said. He reached out and took one of my hands and held it. "I owe you one."

"Why don't you move back into your old place?" I said. "You need somewhere permanent to live."

He shook his head slowly. "I don't think I'm ready for that. I'd be down there wondering if you were up here, if that guy was up here with you . . ."

"I'm so sorry about that, Nick. But I thought—"

"You have nothing to be sorry about," he said. "I probably would have done the same thing you did." He thought a moment. "No, that's not true. I would have done worse. I would have freaked out." He let go of my hand. "It's not your fault. It's probably best if we both just move on."

Half of me wanted to say, "No, the best thing would be for us to get back together." The other half of me felt an obligation to Ben. I had told him Nick was out of my life. I had told him he had nothing to worry about. He had stuck by me even when Nick showed up again. How could I tell him it was over between us? Was I even sure that's what I wanted? Nick made my heart race, but he was hot-tempered and did things that got him into trouble. Ben was deliberate and even-tempered and never got into trouble. That meant something, didn't it?

Nick stood up. Orion jumped eagerly to his feet.

"I'll see you around, Robyn," Nick said. He bent and kissed me lightly on the cheek. The effect was electric. I wanted him to hug me and never let go. But he didn't. He turned, keeping Orion close to him, and let himself out. I sat on the couch and listened to his footsteps fade in the stairwell.

That night as I lay in bed, I told myself that I had done the right thing. I was being true to Ben, who had been true to me. Besides, Nick had had plenty of opportunities to tell me how he felt. If he'd wanted me back, he could have said so. Instead, he'd let me go. Willingly.

Maybe Morgan had been right all along. Maybe Ben really was the one for me. But if that was true, why, when I closed my eyes that night and pictured myself walking on a snowy day, did I see myself hand in hand with Nick?

CHECK OUT THE NEXT BOOK IN THE
ROBYN HUNTER MYSTERIES SERIES:

CHANGE OF HEART

"Robbie," my dad said. "You told me yourself how Billy has been behaving. And you know the case against him—he had a grudge against the victim, he was found with the weapon, he was at the scene. Motive, method, opportunity."

ROBYN HUNTER MYSTERIES

#1 *Last Chance*

Robyn's scared of dogs—but she agrees to spend time at an animal shelter anyway. Robyn learns that many juvenile offenders also volunteer at the shelter—including Nick D'Angelo. Nick has a talent for troublemaking, but after his latest arrest, Robyn suspects that he might be innocent. And she sets out to prove it. . . .

#2 *You Can Run*

Trisha Hanover has run away from home before. But this time, she hasn't come back. To make matters worse, Robyn blew up at Trisha the same morning she disappeared. Now Robyn feels responsible, and she decides to track Trisha down. . . .

#3 *Nothing to Lose*

Robyn is excited to hang out with Nick after weeks apart. She's sure he has reformed—until she notices suspicious behavior during their trip to Chinatown. Turns out Nick's been doing favors for dangerous people. Robyn urges him to stop, but the situation might be out of her control—and Nick's. . . .

#4 *Out of the Cold*

Robyn's friend Billy drags her into volunteering at a homeless shelter. When one of the shelter's regulars freezes to death on a harsh winter night, Robyn wonders if she could've prevented it. She sets out to find about more about the man's past, and discovers unexpected danger in the process. . . .

#5 *Shadow of Doubt*

Robyn's new substitute teacher Ms. Denholm is cool, pretty, and possibly the target of a stalker. When Denholm receives a threatening package, Robyn wonders who's responsible. But Robyn has a mystery of her own to worry about: What's with the muddled phone message she receives from her missing ex-boyfriend Nick?

#6 *Nowhere to Turn*

Robyn has sworn that she's over Nick. But when she hears he needs help, she's too curious about why he went missing to say no. Nick has been arrested again, and the evidence doesn't lean in his favor. When Robyn investigates, she discovers a situation more complicated than the police had thought—and more deadly. . . .

#7 *Change of Heart*

Robyn's best friend Billy has been a mess ever since her *other* best friend Morgan dumped him. To make matters worse, Morgan started dating hockey star Sean Sloane right afterward. Billy is a vegetarian and an animal rights activist—he wouldn't hurt a fly. But when Sean winds up dead on the ice, Billy becomes the prime suspect. Can Robyn prove her friend's innocence?

ABOUT THE AUTHOR

Norah McClintock is the author of several mystery series for teenagers, and a five-time winner of the Crime Writers of Canada's Arthur Ellis Award for Best Juvenile Crime Novel. McClintock was born and raised in Montreal, Quebec. She lives in Toronto with her husband and children.